Unveiled Amish : A Collection of Amish Romance

Sabrina Vicks

Published by Trellis Publishing, 2021.

This is a work of fiction. Similarities to real people, places, or events are entirely coincidental.

UNVEILED AMISH : A COLLECTION OF AMISH ROMANCE

First edition. July 7, 2021.

ISBN: 979-8224345519

Written by Sabrina Vicks.

UNVEILED AMISH

SABRINA VICKS

AN AMISH WINTER

Chapter 1: A Fresh Start

Sarah reached for her bonnet which had dropped from her bed to the floor during her restless sleep. She couldn't remember her dreams once she woke up, but the feeling of dread which accompanied her was slow to move from her body. She sat on the edge of the bed and studied the wall of her room carefully. It was an empty wall, no pictures to adorn it. No posters hung to cover up the holes left by angry fists.

She stood up from her bed and a wave of dizziness overtook her and she had to sit back down for fear of fainting. Inhaling deeply, she lifted herself once more from the bed and steadied herself against the wall. She had been like this for over week, but she refused to call in the doctor for a consultation.

Walking into the kitchen of her new home, she began preparing her breakfast—a simple meal of bread and porridge. She nibbled it thoughtfully as she considered what she might do this morning. It was Monday, so she would not be going into town to sell her quilts. She decided to take a walk along the riverside and explore her new community.

As she made her way down the steps of her house, she heard someone calling out her name. Sarah looked up and saw a young woman running up to her with an older woman in tow.

"Sarah!" the young girl called out. "Oh, I am so glad to finally meet you. I have been trying to introduce myself to you properly since you moved here, but I can never seem to find you at home. I'm Rebecca." The young girl smiled at her warmly and Sarah walked down the last step and extended her hand out to the women. Rebecca took it in hers and smiled as they shook.

"Hello, Sarah," the older woman said, having finally caught up with Rebecca. "My name is Esther. This is my daughter, Rebecca, although I'm afraid you have already learned that information."

Sarah smiled at the pair of them and said, "I am glad to meet both of you. I am sorry for the trouble you have had trying to introduce yourselves! I work often in the markets as I sell my quilts and when I am not there, well, usually I am taking a walk and getting fresh air."

"You mean to say that you go into town to sell your quilts?" Rebecca asked, shocked by Sarah's admission.

"Yes," Sarah nodded. "It seems peculiar, but it is much more lucrative and as I live by myself, I have only myself to rely on."

Sarah saw Rebecca and Esther share a knowing look and Sarah's own smile seemed to slide from her face. This community had been open to her and welcomed her in with open arms, but they still held to certain standards that Sarah knew she would never fulfill. She knew that to them, she was an unmarried woman who traveled into town by herself to make money. The idea sounded entirely too progressive, but Sarah also knew that she would never have it any other way. She had lived another life fulfilling the expectations of others and all it had brought her was misery.

"Well, I do suppose we should be heading back home," Esther said finally once the silence had breached dangerously on the side of being uncomfortable. Sarah nodded and the two women quickly retreated down the path from where they had come from. Sarah saw Rebecca glance furtively back in her direction before quickly turning her around.

Sarah began her walk much as she did every morning since she had arrived in this town. The river beside her bubbled up and triumphed over the smallest obstacles which stood in its way. Every pebble and branch it overcame, she could hear the rejoice in its movement. Sarah sat down beneath a tree and bowed her head in prayer.

She gave thanks to the Lord for all the guidance He had offered her in her life. She prayed to Him to show her kindness and to allow her to live peacefully in her new community. She wanted only to live as simply as possible and she swore to devote herself to Him fully.

"And please, Lord," Sarah whispered quietly, "watch over Jacob and show him the same love and mercy that you have always shown me." She looked up and saw a small rabbit in the distance, his ears perking up as though he heard her prayer. She smiled to herself as she thought about the wonder of God and how one could find Him in everything they saw.

Sarah continued her walk and before she knew it, she had reached the end of the community. She was about to turn back the same path which she had come, but in a curious moment of spontaneity, she decided to try a new path.

She walked through the fields which lay on the border of the community and she admired the crops which they were growing. It had been a successful year and Sarah could tell that the harvest was nearly upon them. Walking without a definitive purpose, Sarah lost herself in reverie.

She began the day dream peacefully as she imagined a young boy running through the fields crying out in glee. She heard herself calling out to him, "Jacob! Jacob!" He turned and his piercing blue eyes touched her soul. The sky turned dark and all too quickly, rain began to pour from the heavens above. Sarah ran to Jacob and grabbed him by the hand, pulling him through the field. They ran all the way to their home where they stood in the doorway, dripping wet. Sarah looked at Jacob who was still wearing a joyful smile—he had thought their race through the field a game and begged her to go outside again. But she had to refuse him and as much as she hated to see the disappointment on his face, she dreaded something else much more. Sarah ushered Jacob to his room so that he could change into dry clothing, but the petulant child refused to budge as a protest. Just as she reached for him, the front door swung open and his father stepped inside. Jacob ran into his mother's arm. The man stared at them closely and after a moment, he shut the door behind him with a loud bang.

Sarah was pulled from her reverie as she ran into something. No, not something—someone.

"Oh, I am so sorry," she apologized as she took several steps backward. "I was not looking where I was going." She looked up and saw a man standing before her. He wore a small smile and his soft brown eyes gleamed. Sarah could not bring herself to utter another word.

"It happens to me all the time," the man said. "I'm Luke. It's nice to meet you. You must be Sarah?"

"Ye—yes," she stuttered. "How did you know?"

"My sister, Rebecca, has been going on and on about meeting you. She makes it a point to introduce herself to any new members of our community so that you don't feel alone here."

Sarah managed a small smile as she recalled her brief exchange with Rebecca from the morning. "I met your mother as well then, Esther."

"Yes, it is not often that you will find one without the other," he laughed. Sarah studied him carefully—the soft curve of his face, his slightly tanned skin which was shaded by his hat, the striking nose which would have seemed ridiculous on any other face, but for him, it seemed perfectly suitable.

"I should be going," Sarah muttered. She was growing wary of their exchange and although he had been merely kind to her, she knew that all too often, kindness from others came with a price.

Luke nodded at her briefly before returning to his work. Sarah dared one final glance at him as he navigated his fields knowingly and then walked the rest of the way home in a hurry. She closed the door behind her and exhaled a breath she hadn't even realized she'd been holding.

Sarah spent the remainder of the day working on a new quilt which she hoped to bring into the market to sell by this week. She toiled away, focusing on each stitch and expertly handled the needles. This was a form of prayer for her as well as she strongly believed that God worked through her hands and with Him as her guidance, they created beautiful works of art.

She put down her newest quilt and walked to the space where she stored all her quilts. From the lowest shelf, she pulled out a small blue quilt which she had made. She brushed her fingers gently over the small white letters which spelled the name Jacob. Closing her eyes, she brought the quilt up to her face and inhaled. It still smelled like him, a familiar scent of grass and boyhood. She thanked the Lord once again for allowing her to experience true joy with Jacob, even if it was ever so brief.

Sarah replaced the quilt on its shelf and closed the door. She walked into her bedroom and after removing her shoes and bonnet, she laid down in her bed and closed her eyes. She willed herself to sleep a dreamless sleep, but alas, like waves on the ocean, dreams came crashing down upon her and she could only pray that the Lord would not let her drown before she awoke.

Chapter 2: The Marketplace

Sarah awoke the next morning just as the sun peeked her head over the horizon. As she moved about the house, preparing for her day at the marketplace, the light slowly spilled in, bathing her in the glorious colors which had always inspired her. She stopped for a moment and whispered a thank you to the Lord.

Sarah had always been a pious woman—she believed strongly in the power of her faith and she knew with certainty, that the Lord had a plan for her. She struggled, however, when it came to others. It was not that she believed that the Lord cared for her more than others or that she was in any way more important, she just believed that in this life, people would act against God more often than not. They would reject His plan for their lives and they would try to bring down those around them as well.

This plagued her as she set up her stand in the marketplace. Many offered her assistance, but she refused any help, determined to succeed only with the help of the Lord. She found herself standing in the marketplace with most of her quilts spread out when a sudden rush of dizziness hit her once again. She swayed to the side and tried to place her hand against the station to steady herself, but she caught hold of a quilt and they began to fall together.

Someone caught her by the arms just as she was about to hit the floor. She squeezed her eyes shut and then opened them as the person lifted her to her feet. She turned and came face to face with Luke.

"I see you have a tendency to fall into me," he said with a laugh.

Sarah blushed furiously at his attempt at humor and she took a few cautious steps back. Luke studied her curiously and then asked, "Are you alright, Sarah? You do not look so well."

"Yes, I am fine. Thank you," Sarah said, still struggling to fully recover. Luke bent down to pick up the quilt which had fallen to the floor, but Sarah rushed over and plucked it from his hands. "It is okay, I can set it back in its place."

Luke watched her with a serious expression and it struck Sarah how handsome he was even when he was not smiling. She bent down to pick up the last two quilts and laid them out in their places.

"Did you make all of these?" Luke asked.

"Yes," Sarah smiled as she examined her work. "I started when I was very young and it grew from a hobby to a means of living." Luke smiled at her as she spoke and he was truly overcome with admiration for her beautiful creations.

"I would like to buy one for my mother," he said.

Sarah looked at him with a wary expression. She did not know whether he was sincerely interested in purchasing one of her quilts or if this was some sort of test to prove that she should not be in the market.

"I have a new one I have started," Sarah said slowly. "Once I finish it, I should give it to you as a gift."

"A gift?" Luke asked, unsure of how to interpret her actions. "For what?"

"For helping me today," Sarah smiled and this seemed to put Luke at ease. He nodded and looked over her quilts one final time before he started moving away. Sarah was reluctant to let him go, although she did not know why. "Why are you in the market today?"

Luke turned around and walked back towards her. He opened the satchel which he wore around him and inside, she could see a variety of fresh vegetables which he had picked from his garden.

"I come to the market sometimes when we have a bountiful harvest to sell the surplus food," he explained. "It helps us to buy what we need for the next year." Sarah nodded as she admired the ripe tomato which sat on the top. Luke seemed to pick up on her interest as he pulled that specific tomato from the bag and handed it to her.

"What is this for?" she asked, holding the tomato in her hand.

"It is a gift," Luke smiled. "For falling into me today. Again." He let out a small laugh and Sarah couldn't help but laugh with him. Luke turned from her and walked over to his own booth down the way where he set up all the vegetables on display.

Soon the market was bustling with people and Sarah had many people approaching her and inquiring about the quilts. However, whenever they asked the price, they often frowned at her response and walked away. Was she really asking too much for these handmade quilts?

Another gentleman approached her booth and she observed him from a distance. He wore a simple suit with a red tie and expensive looking shoes. In between his mouth and nose, there was a silly looking mustache. Sarah had always wondered why men should want to grow only mustaches instead of full beards. What was the purpose of them anyway?

His question pulled her away from her thoughts and she asked, "I'm sorry, what did you ask?"

He looked slightly annoyed at the idea of repeating himself, so he spoke slowly to ensure that she would hear every word. "I asked you if these were handmade?"

Sarah nodded and said, "Yes, I have made all of these." The man nodded appreciatively and placed his hand under his chin as he stroked his mustache in thought.

"How much for this one?" he asked. He held up one of her most recent quilts—it was a beautiful patchwork quilt with soft blues and white. It had been inspired by the clouds in the sky and if one looked very carefully at the center piece, there was a small hand.

"This quilt is $350," Sarah said with a small nod. The man looked at her over the quilt and lowered it slowly back to its place on the table.

"I see," he said. "Well, thank you for your time."

Sarah watched as he stepped away from the table and quickly she asked, "How much would you offer for it?" The man stopped walking. He looked from her to the quilt and back to her again.

"I will give you $50 for it," he said. He pulled out his wallet from his pocket and handed her a $50 bill. Sarah did not fail to notice the plethora of other bills he had as well, but she took the money from him and the man smiled at her as she folded the quilt for him and handed it over.

"Thank you," Sarah said quietly.

"No, thank you!" The man walked away and Sarah stared after him. She had spent over $50 just on the materials needed to make that quilt. At this rate, she would never be able to sustain herself. The bustle slowed down and the experience with the man had drained Sarah. She began wrapping up her booth and storing her quilts away.

"How did you do?" Sarah looked up and saw Luke standing there, that familiar smile holding on.

"I did not do well," she said quietly. Luke walked over to her and began helping her fold the quilts. Sarah looked up at him and said, "I really do not need help. I have been doing this by myself for a long time."

Luke nodded, not letting go of the quilt in his hands. "I know you do not need my help, but I am offering it to you anyway. Just because you have been doing something the same way for so long, does not mean you are incapable of change."

Sarah stopped folding and glanced at the man standing before her. She could not help but feel a sort of goodness about him. She did not reply to him, she merely nodded, and the two of them worked together to pack up her quilts. They walked together outside where Luke offered her a ride in his carriage.

Climbing aboard the carriage with her quilts, Sarah felt a sense of calm come over her. Luke climbed up next to her and took the reins in hand and the two of them rode along in a comfortable silence. They could talk about their lives and the world, they could discuss the Lord, and yet, they chose silence. For most, this might suggest a sort of incompatibility, but for Sarah, she started to feel that maybe Luke understood her better than she understood herself.

He dropped her at her house and helped her carry in all of the quilts. Tilting his hat to her, they said their farewells and Sarah sat down, replaying the day she'd had. She picked up her newest quilt and with a renewed determination, she set to finishing it that night.

As she laid down that night, she felt extremely grateful. She thanked the Lord for leading her to this community and for allowing her to find a friend in Luke. She thanked him for helping her sell the quilt in the market. And finally, she asked him to watch over Jacob.

Sarah closed her eyes and drifted off into a deep slumber. She dreamed of the day that Jacob and she ran together through the field in the rain. She held her child in her arms, but this time when the door opened and a man stepped inside, it was Luke standing before them.

Chapter 3: The Doctor

The day began much the same as every other day and Sarah found a sweet comfort in the routine. She rarely acted outside of her schedule, but sometimes a peculiar mood would come over her which would prompt her to do exactly that. She decided not to go to the market on this day and instead, she walked over to Luke's house carrying the new quilt.

She knocked on the door softly and Luke pulled it open. As soon as his eyes landed on her, he blessed her with his sweet smile. She nodded at him and said hello.

She held out the quilt to him and said, "As promised. My gift for you."

Luke took the quilt and opened it, admiring the beautiful colors she had arranged together. "It is beautiful," he said. "My mother will love this. Come in, come in." He pulled the door open and Sarah walked inside, unsure of what she might find.

Rebecca peered at her from behind a wall and Sarah waved at her.

"Sarah!" Rebecca exclaimed, as though they were old friends who had not seen each other in lifetimes. "I am so glad you could find time to stop by. But wait, I thought you work at the markets on these days?"

Sarah nodded and said, "Yes, I usually do. But today, I decided to stay here."

"Well, we are glad you did," Rebecca smiled. Sarah could not determine whether Rebecca's joy was sincere or whether it was manufactured for the sake of her brother. "Esther!" Rebecca called. "You must come see who has visited us!"

Sarah looked at Luke who shook his head at his sister and laughed. Rebecca smiled at him and then her eyes flickered to the wall where she had just emerged. Esther came out from behind the wall and immediately smiled at Sarah when she saw her.

"Oh, Sarah. How wonderful to see you again," Esther said.

"Look, mother. She has made you this quilt." Luke handed his mother the new quilt and she took it and unfolded it. Both women let out small gasps as they looked it over, admiring every detail.

"It's beautiful," Esther said. "Thank you very much for this." Sarah smiled at the two women and looked again at Luke who was wearing a curious expression. "I have a wonderful idea," Esther said suddenly. "Luke, why don't you take Sarah for a walk today? I know she quite enjoys walking along the river, don't you?"

Sarah nodded at this sentiment and considered the idea of having Luke accompany her. To her surprise, his company actually sounded like a wonderful plan.

"Yes, I think that's what we will do," Luke said. He took Sarah's elbow and led her towards the door. Sarah shivered at his touch and Luke let go reflexively, misinterpreting her reaction.

The two women stood in the doorway and waved at them as they walked down the path together. Sarah looked up at Luke and asked, "What is it?"

"Those two have been trying to get me to ask you on a walk since you moved here," Luke laughed. "They are relentless. I told them that you would need time to adjust to your new surroundings and to get your bearings, but once you ran into me in the fields, well. Let's just say I was waiting for the right moment."

Sarah felt a warmth spread through her, touching every piece of her heart which she had thought she had hidden away, never to be seen again. She recalled the meeting between herself and Rebecca and Esther and the thought dawned on her that perhaps the two of them had not been passing judgements of her, but they were trying to gauge her character for Luke.

The two of them walked along the river and talked with each other amiably. "Your sister and mother both seem very nice," Sarah observed. "Does your father also live there?"

Luke shook his head. "No, my father passed away just before Rebecca was born."

Sarah nodded. "My mother passed when I was young," Sarah explained. "She was giving birth to my younger sister, but there were complications and neither of them survived."

Luke listened to her as she spoke and nodded his head thoughtfully. "It is curious at times when we ponder why loved ones are taken from us. We know that it is all in the Lord's plan, we know that whatever He has planned for us includes learning to grow from these experiences. But still, one does wonder for a reason sometimes."

Sarah shook her head. "No, I trust in His plan fully. I will not wonder for something which He does not desire me to know."

Luke observed her and said, "I admire the strength of your faith. I must admit that sometimes I express myself a little too freely, even to those who I do not know very well."

"You shouldn't take what I said as a judgment against your own character," Sarah explained. "I have just been through many trials and the only way I have survived it all was with His strength and guidance."

Luke considered her words carefully and Sarah could tell that he was debating whether to ask about her trials. In the end, he did not push her for more information and Sarah was relieved that she could keep her secret safe with her.

They sat beneath the tree by the river and spoke of the community and the people here. Luke told her that she would make many friends here who would always be more than willing to help her if she ever needed to ask. Sarah could feel him chipping away steadily at the insecurity which had grown within her, the wariness of others, especially of men.

She talked with him about her old community, the families there lived much to themselves. They were taught to lend a helping hand to others, but it seemed as though everyone hesitated when they saw that someone was in trouble.

"Is that why you left?" Luke asked her.

"In part," Sarah replied slowly. The moment had come—would she tell him the truth of her past which haunted her dreams? Could she trust this fragile friendship to withstand such a blow? Sarah looked at Luke and decided that while he might be able to handle the truth, she was not yet ready to deliver it.

"It is getting late," Luke said, realizing that Sarah had grown distant. "We should get back." Sarah nodded and stood from her place beneath the trees. As soon as she stood up, the dizziness came crashing down upon her with such force that her vision grew black and she fainted into Luke's arms.

Luke carried her from the river all the way to the doctor's house. He knocked on the door loudly and the doctor pulled it open, surprised at the scene before him. He ushered Luke inside and instructed him to lie her down on the table. As the doctor gathered some towels, Luke heard Sarah mumbling something. He leaned forward and listened carefully as she mumbled, "Jacob, no. Please, not Jacob."

The doctor gently pushed Luke back from his position and instructed him to wait in the other room while the doctor completed his examination. The doctor opened each one of Sarah's eyelids and studied her eyes with a magnification tool and flashlight. He pressed gently on her stomach and as he was doing this, Sarah stirred.

She looked around the room, but before panic could seize her, the doctor walked up and smiled down at her. "I am the doctor," he said calmly. "It seems that you had fainted while out with Luke today and he brought you in to see me. Can you sit up?"

Sarah nodded and climbed down from the table and sat in one of the chairs. She looked at the doctor as he studied her carefully.

"You are Sarah, is that correct? You recently joined our community." Sarah nodded and the doctor smiled at her. "Well, it's nice to meet you, although it may have been nicer under different circumstances."

Sarah managed a weak laugh and then coughed. "Is there something wrong with me?" she whispered to him. "This is not the first time I have been dizzy, although it is the only time I have fainted."

"Sarah, may I ask a question which you may find difficult to answer? Please know that I am only trying to gather more information to help you."

Sarah nodded.

"Were you married in your previous community?"

Sarah was shocked by his question—she knew that he had stated it would be difficult to answer, not impossible. She opened her mouth to speak, but no words came out. The doctor waited patiently for her to recover herself.

Finally, Sarah nodded and said, "Yes."

The doctor looked at her matter-of-factly and said to her, "And the man, he was violent towards you?"

Tears sprang to Sarah's eyes as her walls came crashing down around her. This poor doctor, meeting her for the first time and yet able to identify all of her deepest and darkest secrets.

"You don't need to respond to that, Sarah. I know the answer from your reaction," the doctor sighed. "You were with child, Sarah. But soon, he or she will pass from your womb."

Sarah touched her stomach reflexively as a new bout of tears overcame her. She had not even known about the life within her and yet, the sudden sense of loss was overwhelming.

"I cannot tell you how long, Sarah. However, I can tell you with certainty that whatever harm came to you, that is also what came to your unborn child. It could not be withstood." The doctor spoke slowly and the words exchanged between them made Sarah feel as though her head was in a cloud. His voice became muffled and she hardly noticed when Luke came into the room.

"Sarah? Are you okay?" he asked.

She looked up at Luke and shook her head. "Please, take me home." Luke took her by the hand and said goodbye to the doctor. They walked home in silence although Sarah knew that Luke wanted to know what had happened.

Sarah walked up the steps to her house and before she walked inside, Luke said to her, "I am not sure what has happened, but I hope you are okay. Remember, God has a plan for us all, but you do not have to be alone during this time."

At his words, Sarah turned around and Luke could see the sadness in her eyes. He did not want to press her for information she did not want to give him, but he was also unsure of what to say to her that might offer any sort of hope.

She sat down on the steps and after a few moments, Luke joined her. They sat together in silence for a while before Sarah finally spoke.

"I left my other community because my husband would have killed me if I had stayed," she said softly. She could feel Luke straighten beside her and she turned to look in his direction to judge his reaction. "Do you think this makes me a bad person?"

"Why do you believe that, Sarah? Why do you say he would have killed you?"

"Because," Sarah whispered, "he killed our son." Sarah went on to explain the incident where she and Jacob had been running through the field in the rain. She told Luke how when her husband had come home, he was so upset to find the house wet from the two of them. He pushed Sarah to the ground while she was clutching on to Jacob. He was barely two years old at that time. Her husband pulled her up by her hair and threw her against the well and she had hit her head so hard, she could hardly see straight. All she could see was that he was reaching for Jacob who was crying on the floor. All she could do was beg for his mercy, but he had none to give. He threw his son against the wall with such force that Sarah heard a sickening crack. She crawled over to where her son lay on the ground, but he did not move.

"I couldn't stay there," Sarah said between tears. "I have begged God for forgiveness and I truly believe he led me here so that I could start over."

"Sarah," Luke took her hand in his and pressed against his forehead. He looked up at her with such a fierce expression and said, "Sarah, you are safe here. We will not ever let anything hurt you. I will not ever let anything hurt you. Do you hear me?"

Sarah nodded her head and brushed the stray tears from her face.

"I think I will go lie down," she said softly. Luke watched her as she stood from her spot and walked inside, closing the door quietly behind her.

He had heard the doctor earlier—she had been with child and because of what that man had done, she had lost it. He had been the reason she lost two children. Luke could not bear the idea of someone harming Sarah and he struggled with this as he walked home and he wondered, not for the first time, why God had chosen such a difficult path for such a gracious woman.

As Luke walked inside of his house, both his sister and mother were waiting to question how his walk went, but after seeing his expression, they each retreated quietly to the kitchen. Luke went into his own bedroom and put his head against the pillow.

He reached for the bible which he kept by his bed and flipped open to a chapter in Romans. His eyes scanned the page and then landed on this passage, "Not only so, but we also glory in our sufferings, because we know that suffering produces perseverance; perseverance, character; and character, hope. And hope does not put us to shame, because God's love has been poured out into our hearts through the Holy Spirit, who has been given to us."

And suddenly Luke understood. Sarah had been chosen for such a path because she would be able to rise above it—rise above it and cast the light of her faith onto others, giving hope to those who had forgotten the word.

Chapter 4: Beginnings

The following morning Luke walked to Sarah's house before the sun had fully risen. He could not wait to tell her what had happened to him the previous night.

He walked up to her door and knocked softly. He waited patiently and right when he was going to knock again, Sarah opened the door. Her face was flushed, no doubt wondering who could be at her house at such an hour. Luke stole a moment to really appreciate her beauty—her chestnut brown hair peeking out from beneath her hastily placed bonnet and her hazel eyes which looked greener than brown in the early morning light.

"Luke, what are you doing here so early?"

"I had to come see you, Sarah. I was so vexed by your story yesterday, and I could not understand why it would happen to someone like you. I continued to think about what you had said to me earlier in the day—that you do not want to know information which the Lord does not share with you. And I was trying to follow the same thought process as you showed me, but I couldn't. So, I reached for my bible in search of the answer. And look! This is what he showed me." Luke handed her his bible and pointed to the passage which he had read the night before.

He watched Sarah as she read it and he could see her familiar light reigniting within her heart.

"Luke," Sarah said slowly. "I think that I was meant to meet you. I believe the Lord sent you into my life in my darkest hour to ensure that I would not lose faith."

Luke nodded and took Sarah's hand in his own. "And you," he said. "He sent you into my life so that you might restore the hope in my own heart." Sarah smiled at Luke and descended the steps. Together, they traced her favorite path along the river and she told Luke about the triumphant song of the river as it passed over the obstacles it was presented with.

Luke looked at Sarah and said, "Listen closer, Sarah. That is *your* song."

A PROPER AMISH MAN

ABBY BARNES

Abigail knew the path to the Church by heart. She could walk it blindfolded if she had to. Once, her brother Eli had dared her to. She made it halfway before she tripped on a rock and sprained her wrist. Everyone laughed, but she argued it could have happened to anyone.

She remembered her mother, red faced, her thick, black hair slipping from her bonnet when she discovered what her middle daughter had done. *"Dat is niet wat de dames doen!"* That is not what ladies do.

She continued to walk the path every day, sometimes twice a day. That was what ladies did in Amish country; they went to church. Usually Abigail was accompanied by one of the little ones. She was one of eleven: Mary was the eldest, then Ruth, Miriam, Eli, Aaron, herself, Samuel, Isaac, Hannah, Sarah and then finally Baby Jilly who had accompanied her that day.

Jilly held Abigail's hand as she skipped down the path. Her black hair was in two braids on either side of her head, and her boots were worn from the six little girls that had worn them before her. Abigail figured she should have scolded Jilly for skipping, *dat is niet wat de dames doen,* but as she wasn't her mother she figured she would let her get away with it.

"What are we gonna sing today?" Jilly asked her big sister. She was five. Abigail was sixteen.

"I'm not sure," she said. "Whatever Pastor John has planned for us, I guess."

"Ik hoop dat het iets leuk om te zingen," Jilly said, accidentally slipping into the Dutch their parents spoke at home, and whenever they were talking with other elders in the town. *I hope it's something fun to sing,* Jilly had said.

Deep in her gut, Abigail had the impulse to correct her; tell her that speaking Dutch would only drag her further into the community, and that she would never be able to escape. However, she could not poison her baby sister's mind.

Her poison was off in the distance. A few months before, her community had opened their gates to tourists coming to examine Amish life. It was a controversial topic among members of the community, and a good chunk of the men had voted against it, but the majority won. There was a school group there, of boys and girls about Abigail's age. As her and Jilly walked closer, she was able to examine them more. She was envious of the girls with short hair, cut to their chins, and the paint on their face that she would never be allowed to wear. The boys had shaggy hair, and were cute; unlike men in the town. Except perhaps Lucas . . .

"OMG she's so cute!" one of the girls pointed to Jilly as they walked by. "Look at her little dress!"

Jilly, like a good little Amish girl, ignored them. They were sinners after all. And following in her sister's example, Abigail did the same.

****

The church was a one room building in the center of town. The old white stone was drafty, as many of the buildings that Abigail visited, without a fire burning except in the coldest of winters. Her and Jilly bowed their heads as the entered, and then walked over to the piano where Pastor John sat.

"Good morrow, girls," he said. Pastor John was old, about fifty or so, with whiting hair and lines around his mouth. He was easily the kindest man in the whole community. He had come to them as a teen from the outside world. His parents had died in a fire, and his brother and him ran away from their foster parents. They found solace in the community, and after a few years were baptised. Pastor John became a pastor. His elder brother became Abigail and Jilly's father.

"Hello, Uncle John!" Jilly beamed.

Pastor John laughed. "How about some hymns?"

They warmed up first. Jilly still had a baby voice, but as the youngest walking member of the community she warmed the hearts of the elders whenever she sang in church. Abigail, however, had a gorgeous voice. As they sang their praises to God and Jesus, there was a creak of the door opening, and the steps of people walking inside.

The first thought Abigail had was that the school group was not allowed to be inside of the church; they were sinners, and they would taint the building. Pastor John did not seem to mind, however, and Abigail just continued singing, trying to tune out Jilly's baby squeaks and the sounds of the teenagers whispering. She accidentally glanced over at them once, and saw a blonde haired girl there front and center smiling. Uncomfortable, Abigail looked away, back at Pastor John.

The teenagers left eventually, to most likely go play with the baby sheep that had just been born, and their lesson ended as well. The girls thanked their uncle the pastor, and began their walk home.

****

Lucas was the shepherd's son. He lived next door to Abigail's family farm, which was about a half a mile away. He was the eldest, the only boy with seven sisters. He had a steady future, with no threats to his family's welfare. He was good looking, strong, and a man of God.

As Abigail was exactly the same age as Lucas, it was no secret that they would be pushed together at some point. She fought it forever, making it a point to torture Lucas when they were children. She had pushed him into the river once, ruining his clothes and nearly breaking his arm. She remembered her mother that day vividly: *dat is niet wat de dames doen!*

However, the more she tried to fight it, the more her feelings for Lucas grew more and more, until eventually she felt as though she was going to burst. Of course, being a lady, she was not allowed to tell him.

About a week before that mentioned singing lesson with Jilly, a letter that had been addressed to her was tucked into the chicken coop. She had discovered it when she went to fetch the family's eggs that morning.

She couldn't read it in front of Hannah, Sarah or Jilly as she knew they would tell her parents. She tucked it into her apron, and impatiently waited until she had a moment alone.

That moment came when she went to go check on their cow, Miss Lavinia, who was due to give birth at any day. She hid inside the barn, completely alone, and practically tore open the letter Lucas had written her:

My dearest Abigail,

As a proper Amish man, I should be writing this letter in Dutch, however I just cannot bring myself to do that. This town has us restricted in so many ways, but fortunately it seems that it is completely alright with the two of us being together. I did not want to alarm you, but I wanted to tell you that this evening I will be meeting with your father and I will be asking to court you. I hope this is okay, yet in my heart I know that it will be. I know you love me as I love you, and I am looking forward to this journey together. Now as a proper Amish man, I must say this: Ik hou van jou. I love you!

Lucas

Abigail had nearly cried when she had read the letter. Her darling Lucas . . . he was actually hers!

That night, just as he had promised, he came by right after they finished their dinner. He asked to speak with Abigail's father, Pastor John's brother, who was named Ethan. Ethan was a large man; bred in the outside world but easily adapted to life within the community. Had Abigail not been told of her father's past she never would have guessed it. The three littles ones (Sarah, Hannah and Jilly) were unaware.

Lucas was tall as well, with broad shoulders that were good for carrying injured sheep. He had sandy colored hair and bright blue eyes that lit up his entire face. Abigail tried not to melt when she walked into their home.

"Lucas!" Jilly and Sarah, who was a year older than her, ran over to him and gave him a hug. Abigail expected a scolding from their mother, but then quickly remembered she was rather soft on the two little ones.

"Hello to the two most beautiful little ladies," Lucas said, returning the hug. He then extended his hand to Ethan and shook it.

The two had excused themselves. Abigail, pretending she did not know what was going on, helped her mother with the dishes, all the meanwhile trying to hide the fact that her knees were clacking together with nerves. After what felt like hours, her father poked his head into the doorway.

"Abigail," he said. "A moment, please."

"You're in trouble!" Sarah taunted.

"Mind your manners," their mother said.

Abigail thought that if her father was asking her to go outside that was a good sign. Wasn't it? She wiped her wet hands on her apron and excused herself. It was beginning to be cool.

"Lucas." She nodded her head.

"Miss Abigail." He smiled.

Ethan shut the door. "Abigail, Lucas here has asked for my permission to court you. I have said yes, but as I am not a man of stone I wanted to know if that would be alright with you."

Abigail pretended to think for a second, but she was so happy she could not stand it. A smile burst out of her. "Yes!" she squealed.

Ethan laughed, and then patted Lucas on the shoulder. "Make sure to take care of her now," he said. "She may not be my eldest daughter, nor my youngest, but she still means the world to me."

Abigail and Lucas nodded their heads to each other, as that was what a courtship entailed, but Abigail had a feeling that wasn't going to last.

****

After dinner that night and after everyone went to bed, Abigail slipped out the bedroom window to the barn. If she was caught, she would tell her parents she was checking on Miss Lavinia, when in fact she was going to meet Lucas.

He was petting Miss Lavinia, who still had yet to give birth. "She might be having twins," he said, as Abigail entered the barn.

"You're never supposed to insult a woman's weight," Abigail mused.

"In a good way," Lucas said, smiling. "Twins means more money. More dairy. More beef."

Abigail shuttered. "They're not even born yet and you want to send them off to slaughter?"

"In the outside world, they have people who don't eat meat," Lucas said. "Because they can afford to do stuff like that."

Abigail pet Miss Lavinia's snout, and the cow, uncomfortable, closed her eyes and allowed herself to be soothed. "Ever think about leaving the community?" she asked.

"And being shunned?" Lucas scoffed, but his face read that he wasn't completely opposed to the idea. "Where would we go?"

Abigail shrugged. "Somewhere big," she said. "Like . . . Philedelphia. Or New York City. Or Hong Kong!"

Lucas laughed. "Hong Kong is in a different country."

"But we could never go there if we didn't leave," Abigail said. Miss Lavinia opened her eyes and gave her a sorrowful look. "We would be trapped here forever, narrowing our world, not seeing everything. Don't you want to see everything?"

"Do you never want your parents to speak to you again?" Lucas asked.

"I wouldn't mind," Abigail said, which was the half truth.

"What about Jilly?"

To that, Abigail had to be more creative. "We would take us with her!"

"Your parents wouldn't be okay with that and you know it."

Abigail felt defeated. Miss Lavinia mooed, and it sounded painful. She was sure to be in labor soon, if not beginning to already. Before Abigail could tell Lucas this discovery, his arms were wrapped around her waist.

She turned around into his kiss. It wasn't the first time he had kissed her. Though pre marital *anything* was against the rules, the two of them were relaxed when it came to kissing. There was no way that everyone who kissed someone else ended up in hell, and the two of them agreed not to progress it any further. But sometimes, like moments like that, when he literally knocked the breath right out of her, Abigail found it hard to resist.

"I wish we could leave," he whispered, when he paused.

"Neither of us are baptised," she replied. "We could and if we didn't like it -"

"I'm the only son."

Abigail didn't say anything. She knew how much of a struggle that would be for him. It would be a struggle for her too, even though she had plenty of brothers and was not the sole heir to her family's farm. She looked at Miss Lavinia. She would miss her, and her siblings, especially little Jilly, but she did not know if she could miss the community life. The problem was it was not a revolving door; the only ticket out was a strict one-way.

"Well," she said. "We will figure something out."

Lucas didn't reply. He just held her tight.

****

About a week later, Miss Lavinia had given birth to a new calf. It was a boy. Jilly named him Jedidiah, because she felt like that was a good name for a cow. A day after she gave birth, Abigail found herself headed down the familiar path to the church with Jilly, to their weekly lesson.

When they got there, however, they did not find a lonely Pastor John; they discovered he was with someone else. He was tall, taller than Lucas and Ethan, with bright blonde hair to his shoulders. What struck Abigail the most was that he was wearing outside world clothing.

"Hello, Abigail. Jilly," Pastor John said. "This is Mac McMullan."

Mac. That wasn't a name, was it? Abigail nodded politely and said, "How do you do?" Jilly didn't say anything. She didn't understand the difference between who she was allowed and who she was not allowed to talk to, so she reserved herself to not talking to anyone.

"I'm well," Mac said. He had a high pitched voice, and a little bit of a lisp. "You must be the talented Abigail that I have heard so much about."

Abigail was taken aback. "How did you hear about me?"

"My sister was on a trip here a week back," Mac explained. "With her friends from school, and she heard you sing. I reached out to Pastor John about maybe coming to meet you, and he said that was okay. So I was actually wondering . . ." He furrowed his eyebrows together and grinned. "Do you think you could maybe sing to me? A little?"

"I don't know anything besides hymns," Abigail said, a little bit embarrassed. "That's probably not what you listen to where you're from."

"Whatever makes you happy!" Mac grinned. "Lucy said you were amazing at whatever you were doing, so I totally want to hear it."

Lucy. That was a more normal name. Abigail distinctly remembered the little blonde girl that was pointing to her when her and Jilly were singing the week before. That must have been Lucy.

Pastor John sat at the piano, and Jilly and Abigail circled around him. Abigail noticed her little sister had her back turned to Mac, and had a strong urge to tell her not to be rude, but she couldn't bring herself to do it.

Pastor John played the beginning chords to *In the Garden of Eden.* Abigail began to sing. Out of the corner of her eye she looked at Mac, who had his arms folded across his chest and a huge smile on his face. His look made her feel more confident, and she smiled as she continued to sing.

When the hymn was over, Jilly crinkled her nose together. "I don't know if I like that one."

Pastor John didn't get a chance to reply; Mac began clapping as he walked over to the girls. "That was beautiful," he said. "Really. Beautiful. Abigail, you're amazing."

"Jilly too," Abigail said, because even though she wouldn't speak to this man, she knew her baby sister's feelings were hurt.

Mac nodded, a smile still on his face. "Jilly too."

"Is it everything you expected?" Abigail teased.

"Everything and more," Mac said, looking at Pastor John. "Which is why I am here. I am a music producer. I work for a predominantly Christian label in New York City."

New York City was a solid seven hours away from where Abigail's community was. She couldn't even imagine what it looked like; only that it was a huge city of the outside world. She heard they had buildings that reached the sky and trains underground. She would be swallowed in New York City.

"Label?" Abigail asked.

"Music label," Mac clarified. "And I think you might be our next solo artist. If you're up to it."

"Does my mamma and papa know you're here?" Jilly asked Mac, momentarily forgetting that she wasn't supposed to talk to him . . . technically.

Abigail looked at Pastor John. He looked guilty. Clearly he knew about Mac and his intentions, but did not bother to tell his brother. Abigail in turn felt a little guilty, but at the same time tried to imagine what could happen in a big city like New York. She would be able to sing for the label, and wouldn't be constricted to bonnets and shunning strangers.

And then she thought of Lucas . . .

"No," Mac finally answered Jilly. "But I would love to meet them."

"You can't come inside," Jilly said. "You could ruin our house."

"Let's not be too hasty," Abigail said, a little embarrassed at her sister's behavior. "Papa would most likely like to speak to you though," she continued, talking to Mac.

Mac looked at his watch on his wrist. "Well, I actually have to scoot today. I'm meeting with another Amish girl a little north of here, but yeah! Definitely tomorrow? How does that sound?"

Abigail looked at Pastor John. He nodded. "Sounds good," he said. "I'll talk to my brother tonight. Prepare him."

****

Abigail prayed Jilly wouldn't say anything over dinner about Mac. Fortunately, the little one seemed to know when she could tell things to her parents when she couldn't, so she stayed quiet. The entire time they were eating, Abigail's knees were shaking. She kept looking at her mother to see if she knew anything. Not that Pastor John had the chance to tell her, but sometimes Abigail was convinced her mother could read minds.

She wanted to move to New York City. She wanted to sing for Mac, and have fans, and be in the outside world. She was so excited, but so scared at the same time. She would be leaving her entire life behind, and she would not be able to come back. She looked at her brothers and sisters, and even her parents, and tried to imagine her life without them. She couldn't.

Yet at the same time, she imagined the outside world. She could do so much. She wouldn't be restricted to the tiny little community, and she could be with the modern times. She could wear pants. She could let her hair down and even cut it shorter if she wanted to. There were so many possibilities, yet she was so scared.

She kept yearning for Lucas. After dinner, once everyone was in bed, Abigail once again slipped out of the window and went to the barn. Miss Lavinia was there, along with Jedidiah. The baby looked exactly like his mother; cream colored with brown spots. He even had the same shape one covering his right eye. And right next to the calf, petting him on the head, was Lucas.

"Hey," he said.

"I got asked to record an album in New York City," Abigail blurted out, because she was scared if she held it in any longer she was going to explode.

Lucas stopped petting Jedidiah, and looked at Abigail. She couldn't tell what exactly he was thinking. "You . . .is this a joke?"

"Do I look like I'm joking?" she winced.

He looked back at Jedidiah, and began petting the little calf on his head. Abigail thought he may have been crying, but she wasn't too sure. The barn wasn't very well lit.

"You're leaving."

"I never said that," she replied.

"But you want to. Otherwise you never would have said anything to me."

Lucas looked up, and instantly Abigail felt heart broken. His eyes were swelling up with tears.

"I don't know," she said, and she began to break.

Before she knew it, he was kissing her. And she was kissing him back, pulling his hair and pressing her lips into his. How could she give this up? How could she move far away from him?

She didn't know what to do.

When he broke away, she was crying as well. Lucas wiped away his tears with his right thumb, his left hand still holding her face. "If you leave, you'll be shunned."

"I haven't been baptized yet," Abigail said. "Neither have you. We can come back. We don't have to leave forever."

"They'll never look at us the same."

"Your parents love you."

"That doesn't mean they'll support me." Lucas' hands fell away. "That doesn't mean they'll ever forgive me for putting their sheep and their livelihood in jeopardy."

"Maybe they'll have another baby?" Abigail offered, even though she acknowledged she was just being desperate. "A boy?"

"They can't control that."

Abigail understood that no matter what she said, she would not be able to make Lucas feel better. He left a few minutes later, and all she could do was try and figure out whether or not she was ready for this.

Before she could even try to say anything, the barn door opened. Lucas and Abigail sprung apart, and Abigail expected it to be either of her parents, and was surprised to see her brother Eli. He was eighteen, twins with Abigail's brother Aaron, and a hardworking man of Jesus.

"Eli . . ." she began. This was almost worse than being caught by her father.

He had a stern look on his face. "I came to check on Miss Lavinia," he said, and he looked at Lucas. "You should go."

Lucas left without any hesitation, leaving the two siblings alone. "This isn't what it looks like . . ." Abigail said.

"Were you having sex?" Eli asked.

Abigail shook her head. "Nothing like that." She bowed her head, ashamed. "I have been asked to leave the community, to sing for a music label. And I won't go unless Lucas comes with me. And he can't leave his farm because he is the only son. So I don't know what to do."

"You'll be shunned," Eli said.

"I know."

"Do you love him?"

That question caught her off guard. She looked up and stared her brother straight in the eye and said, "Yes."

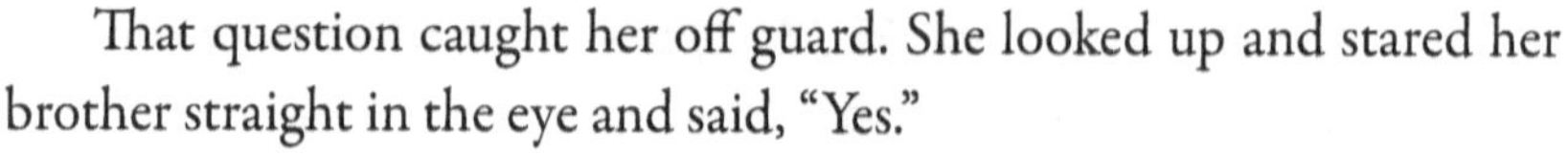

The next morning, after Abigail and the four little ones milked the cows and got the eggs, they met inside their house for breakfast. Abigail helped her mother cook, while everyone else gathered around after doing their morning chores.

Her father had already been into town, and Abigail suspected he had talked to Pastor John. She was worried.

They all sat around the table, bowed their heads in prayer, and began to eat. The little girls began their usual chatter, and Abigail noticed her father kept looking at her. She could feel her stomach churning, but she could not ask him what he was thinking. That would be rude.

She also kept looking at Eli, expecting him to have cracked and told her parents what he had seen last night. Yet somehow, he was remaining cool.

Finally, her father said, "Ik denk dat je moet worden gedoopt, Abigail." *Abigail, I think you should be baptized.*

Abigail swallowed. He knew. She tried to remain calm when she said, "Maar vader, ik ben slechts zestien. Ik heb alles van mijn studie van de Bijbel niet gedaan. Ik ben nog jong." *But father, I am only sixteen. I have not done all my Bible study. I am still young.*

Her father waved his hand, dismissing the entire thing. "Je bent je moeder was dezelfde leeftijd," he said, looking at his wife.

He was right. She was the same age her mother was when she was baptized. Abigail felt that churning in her stomach.

"Lucas," she finally said.

"You're in love, aren't you?" Jilly asked.

"Jilly, uw ontbijten," their mother snapped.

"You know I don't speak Dutch," Jilly said, even though that was a lie. She went back to eating her breakfast like her mother told her to.

"I am not ready to get baptized," Abigail said, using English instead of Dutch. If she was going to be living in the outside world she had to get used to outside language. She also acknowledged that her and Lucas only spoke English to each other. Maybe he wanted to be as rebellious as she was.

She couldn't think about Lucas. Not then anyway. She ate her breakfast, and took in the silence at the table.

****

Later that day, Abigail snuck away. She found Pastor John in the church, sitting in a pew reading a Bible.

"Pastor John," she said. "May I talk to you?"

"Can I just say how relieved I am you asked me that in English?" He smiled warmly.

She sat next to him. Had he not been a man of faith she never would have put herself in the position with him. But most importantly, she needed to know what to do.

"I'm scared," she finally said.

"About Mac's offer?" he asked.

"That," she said. "And my parents now want me to get baptized. And there's Lucas . . ."

She stopped herself then, and felt her cheeks go red.

"Abigail," Pastor John said. "It is alright to fall in love."

"You don't fall in love here," she explained, feeling a little silly having so that that to a prominent member of the community. "You don't fall in love, you court someone your father approves and then you get married. You have sex with someone to reproduce according to what God had told you to do, you do not kiss them because it feels good."

She stopped herself again.

"Have you kissed Lucas?" he asked.

She nodded.

"That's okay," he said. "It is okay to fall in love. And more importantly your parents approve of you falling for him. The outside world is scary, and if you're going to go out there it'll be good for you to bring him with you."

"He won't go," she said, tears coming into her eyes. "He cannot leave the sheep. He is the only son in his family, and if he leaves they will be ruined. He can't do it, and I do not want to be angry with him for it, but I am. I am angry."

"Then you have a choice to make."

"I don't know what to choose. I don't want to be alone."

Pastor John sighed. "You know, in a different life, you would have called me Uncle John. You would have lived in the outside world. You would have been getting ready for your first prom right now, taking pictures with your friends . . . being a normal teenager."

"I always forget you're from out there," Abigail replied.

"You're father is too." Pastor John looked at her. "Your mother may not be able to understand, but he will. We left together and it was the right decision for us. But that doesn't mean you shouldn't be able to find the right decision for you."

"You really think my father will understand?" Abigail had a trace of hope in her voice.

Pastor John nodded. "I really do."

****

That night, Abigail sat with her parents, and Pastor John, and Mac, whom her parents had broken all of the rules and allowed him in the house. He wore a jacket and jeans, and he had tied his hair back into a ponytail. The other kids were away, outside doing chores or playing.

"You want to take my little girl into the city," Ethan said.

"I do," Mac nodded. "She's a talented singer and I believe her voice could be admired by those around the world."

"I grew up in the city," Ethan said. Abigail noticed her mother touch his arm. "I know what that world is like. It's cold and cruel, and here it is safe and nothing harmful will happen to her. If she is baptized, nothing will happen to her when she leaves this world either."

"I want to live, father," Abigail said. "I love you and mamma, and I love everyone here but I don't know what is outside of these walls and I want to learn. I know you think it is cruel and scary, and that life was hard for you when it was young, but why do so many people live out there instead of here? There must be something good there, and Mac can show me, and I can sing about Jesus. I don't want to be here and never know what I could have done. I would hate myself. I want to experience and if I don't like it . . ." She stopped herself.

"You would want to come back," Pastor John finished for her.

"I would want to come back." She nodded.

Before anyone could say anything, the door opened and Eli came in. He nodded, before going over to the bench next to the door to take off his boots. He was muddy; no doubt cleaning the stalls.

"What about Lucas?" It was her mother that asked the question this time.

Abigail felt tears well in her eyes, but she wouldn't dare shed them. "I would miss him terribly. So terribly."

"He could come with you," Mac offered. "I'm down with that."

"Down?" Abigail's mother questioned.

"Okay with that," Mac clarified. "If she wanted to bring him. He could come along."

"He can't leave his farm," Abigail said. "So that's that."

It was then that she noticed her mother was crying. She was dabbing her eyes with a handkerchief, and her nose was running. "Mamma . . ." Abigail began.

"I raised you to be a good Amish girl," her mother cried. "And I want what is best with you, and I feel like I have failed. I feel like I have not made you happy. I feel as though I have not given you a great life."

"Mamma . . ."

Breaking all the rules, Abigail stood up and walked over to her mother and hugged her. "I love you so much," she whispered. "And I'll come back to see you."

"Don't get baptized," her mother whispered back. "I don't want to shun my daughter."

"You don't have to shun me," Abigail said.

It was then that Abigail felt arms around her, and noticed her father was holding her as well. The three of them hugged, and Abigail almost felt completely at peace.

****

Mac had a car. Abigail had seen them before, but she had never ridden in one. This one was red, and it was small, but it looked like it would go fast. She thought of how her life was going to be surrounded by cars now, and she was nervous, but excited. The would be more predictable than horses, right?

Her entire family had gathered to say goodbye. Except Eli, but Abigail did not want to comment on that. Jilly looked annoyed, but her parents promised they would explain to her exactly what was going on. The other little girls looked sad. They had been crying all day.

All of her sisters hugged her goodbye, and her brothers shook her hand. Even her elder sisters, who were all married, had come to send her off with their children and spouses. Her nieces and nephews marveled at the car, and even tried to climb on top of it, before they were pulled away by their parents. Abigail's parents hugged her, and her mother whispered that she loved her in Dutch in her ear. Abigail prayed that she never forgot the language, even though she complained about it sometimes.

"Ready to go?" Mac asked her, and Pastor John. He had agreed to go with her for a week to make sure she settled in okay. That made her parents feel better. Abigail asked if he would be shunned, but since he was returning, it would be excused as a business adventure. He was off to hear about the Lord and he would be back.

Abigail was about to say yes, but down the path she saw two figures running towards them. It took a couple seconds, but she then realized it was Eli and . . .

"Lucas?" she whispered.

They were both out of breath when they reached them. Abigail noticed Lucas had a burlap bag in his hand. "Abigail," he panted.

"We made a deal," Eli explained, a little less out of breath than Lucas. His thick, black hair was sweat soaked, but his face was completely lit up. Abigail almost did not recognize her brother. "We made a deal, I talked to his father . . . I'm marrying Mary."

Mary . . . Lucas' sister . . .

"What?" Abigail asked.

"We've been courting," he explained. "In secret, we've been courting, and I asked her father if I could marry her and that way, I can get the farm and the sheep and Aaron . . . he could take over ours." He looked at his twin. "Is that okay with you?"

Aaron shrugged, and smiled. "I'll take it."

Eli looked at Ethan. "Is that okay with you, Pa?"

Ethan nodded, and then walked over to Lucas. He set his hand on his shoulder. "You take good care of my girl. It's a scary world out there. Don't hurt her. Don't cause her any pain."

Lucas nodded aggressively. "Definitely, sir. Definitely."

"And ask her if she wants you to come," Ethan continued.

Lucas looked at Abigail. "Does this plan work for you?"

Abigail could not imagine a better life. She hugged her father, and then her mother, and then Eli because she was simply out of words. She then got into the car with Mac, Lucas, and Pastor John, driving off to the outside world.

A LEAP OF FAITH

STEPHANIE SWIFT

Hope Miller laced her fingers together on top of her lap and did her best to empty her mind so she could focus on Bishop Abram's sermon.

It wasn't an easy task.

Sitting to her right was her mother and father, both of whom sat with rigid backs and facial expressions as hard and stern as the wooden pew they were seated on. To her left were her aunt Martha and uncle Seth, who both appeared comfortable and at ease, holding hands and smiling as they listened to the message. The two couples couldn't be more opposite if they tried, and she felt like neutral ground between them, which was disconcerting to say the least.

Hope cautiously looked over her right shoulder and smiled at Noah Wyse, her closest friend and ally. He sat a couple of pews behind them on the other side of the sanctuary with his six-year-old daughter, Ivy, who gave her a shy wave when she caught Hope looking their way. She wanted to wave back at her, but she knew if her mother or father caught her goofing off during the service she would never hear the end of it.

Noah gave her a sympathetic smile, and she turned her attention back to Bishop Abram before she made the mistake of smiling back at him and causing an uproar if one of the elders of the church caught her doing it. Even though she and Noah were just friends, it was highly frowned upon in their small Amish community for the unmarried men and women to cavort with each other unless they were promised to marry. It was ridiculous, really, but the last thing she wanted to do was cause a scene.

Hope sighed. If only things were simpler and less complicated. At twenty years old, she was one of the oldest from her generation who hadn't married, but that didn't bother her in the least. After growing up in a home with parents who shared a loveless marriage, a relationship was the furthest thing from her mind. Because of their strict faith, divorce was next to impossible, but there were many times during her youth when she wished her parents would go their separate ways. She couldn't imagine what brought the two of them together, unless it was an arranged courtship, because there was no way to picture them ever being in love.

Her aunt and uncle, on the other hand, were the epitome of love and devotion. You could see it in the way they looked at each other that their love was real. When Hope made the decision to leave home three years prior and move in with her aunt and uncle to help with her quilting business, the relief she felt was overwhelming. Gone were the days stepping on egg shells around her parents and living in a home that was so cold she could feel it in her bones. With Hope being their only child, she could only imagine how depressing the atmosphere must be now that they were alone together, and the thought made her heart ache.

No, she would never get married. Not if it meant she would lose a piece of herself and spend the rest of her days wishing for her freedom. No man was worth that.

Her mother nudged her side, startling her and making her jump. She hadn't realized she'd drifted off into her own little world, but the service was nearly over and every head in the room was bowed as Bishop Abram said his closing prayer. Hope shut her eyes as her cheeks burned hot from embarrassment. As soon as the Bishop said "amen", and everyone started for the door, her mother was on her case.

"Honestly, Hope...do you ever stop daydreaming?" she muttered.

Hope took a deep breath to keep from saying something she regretted. "I'm sorry, mother."

As they stood in line for the door, she glanced around the room in search of Noah and Ivy, but didn't find them. Hope peered through one of the church windows to see if they had already left the church, and she spotted them near a grove of trees with Victoria Kaufmann, a young widow from their area. While Noah and Victoria talked, Ivy played close by on a tire swing hanging from an old oak tree.

The two of them were deep in conversation about something, and when Victoria reached out and touched Noah's arm, Hope's temper bristled in response, which caught her off guard. *What was that about?* she wondered. She and Noah had never been romantically involved, and it wasn't the first time a single woman had flirted with Noah since his wife, Maria, passed away not long after Ivy was born.

"Are you alright?"

Hope looked behind her at her aunt Sadie, who was eyeing her skeptically. "*Yah*. Why do you ask?"

Sadie shrugged and smiled. "You just seemed puzzled for some reason."

Puzzled was putting it lightly, but Hope shook her head to clear her thoughts and to keep from dwelling on it. She and Noah were just friends, and it was probably just her over-protectiveness getting the best of her anyway. She knew very well how desperate some of her single friends were when it came to marriage, and she didn't want to see Noah hurt. That was all. He and Ivy had been through enough.

When they finally made their way outside, Hope and her aunt and uncle followed her parents to their horse and carriage to see them off, and Hope forced herself not to look in Noah and Victoria's direction.

"Sister, we would love for you and William to join us for lunch."

Hope rolled her eyes heavenward. It was the same thing every Sunday, and it always ended the same way - with her parents refusing. She would never understand how her aunt Sadie could be so patient with them when they treated her so callously.

Her mother and father stopped walking and turned to look at them. Her lips were pursed and her roughly chiseled face was set in her usual sour expression. Her father's face held no expression whatsoever.

"*Denki*, Sadie, but I'm afraid we'll have to decline. Hope, may I speak to you in private?"

Hope inhaled sharply and glimpsed at her aunt Sadie, who appeared just as perplexed. It was odd for her mother to want to talk to her about anything, much less alone. When she grabbed Hope's elbow and roughly led her a few feet away, she held her breath, expecting the worst.

"When are you coming home?" her mother asked.

Hope furrowed a brow as she pulled away from her mother's grasp. "What do you mean? I don't plan on moving back home. We've already discussed this."

Her mother huffed and puffed as she crossed her arms haughtily over her chest. "You need to stop being a burden to your aunt and uncle."

Hope took a step back. Her mother was never one to mince words, but her accusation stung. She looked over at her aunt and uncle, who were unsuccessfully trying to pull her father into conversation.

"I'm not a burden to them. How can you say that?"

Her mother wouldn't be swayed. "You're an adult, and you can't live with them forever. It's time for you to grow up and find a husband while there's still time."

Hope blinked twice. "While there's still time? You mean, while I'm still young enough to snag one?"

She didn't want to be disrespectful, but this time her mother was close to crossing the line. There was a significant difference between being concerned and acting downright rude. She hated to consider that she might be right. Did her aunt Martha and uncle Seth really consider her a burden? They'd never said anything about her overstaying her welcome, but perhaps they were just being nice.

Hope felt her eyes sting with hot tears, but she blinked them back, refusing to let her mother see that she'd gotten under her skin. Fortunately, she turned and walked back to the group before Hope had the chance to say anything further, which was probably for the best. The last place she wanted to fight with her was in the church yard with the whole congregation listening in.

She cast a wayward glance in Noah's direction, but he was still busy talking to Victoria Kaufmann and oblivious to everything else. Ivy noticed her right away and gave her a big wave as she swung back and forth on the tire swing with a silly grin highlighting her beautiful little face. Hope waved back before resigning herself to return to her family.

* * * *

Noah leaned slightly to his left so he could peek over Victoria's shoulder, and he felt his blood boil when he saw Hope talking to her mother. Actually, her mother was doing most of the talking, and he could tell from the sullen look on her face that the woman wasn't happy...as usual.

"Noah? Is something wrong?"

Her turned his attention back to Victoria, feeling guilty that he'd let his thoughts roam elsewhere. Victoria was a sweet woman, and even though he had no interest in anything other than friendship, it was obvious she felt differently. It may have been a long time since he was with another woman, but he knew flirting when he saw it.

"I'm so sorry. What were you saying?" he asked.

Victoria touched his arm again, something he noticed she was doing quite frequently while they talked. Any other man may have enjoyed it, but he'd already been blessed with the love of his life, and he wouldn't risk his heart being broken again. Plus, there was his daughter to think about, and he was far more concerned with her well-being than anything else.

"I asked if you were planning on attending the charity auction this Saturday. I'll be donating a picnic lunch."

So that was what she was getting at. It was all perfectly clear now. The auction was being held to raise money toward new books and other materials for their community schoolhouse, and it was tradition for the single women to make picnic lunches to be auctioned off among the single men. The winner would then share the lunch with the woman who donated it.

"*Yah*, I hope I can. It just depends on if I get my orders finished in time."

It wasn't a lie. Being the only blacksmith in the area, there was seldom a weekend that passed where he wasn't busy working overtime to finish orders. Not only did he have orders to complete for his neighbors, but several shop owners in nearby Lancaster were faithful customers too.

"Well, perhaps I'll see you there," she replied.

She gave him a shy smile before she turned and walked away, and Noah expelled a long breath. He stole a glance at Ivy as she played on the tire swing, and his heart swelled twice its size when she grinned back at him. She favored her mother so much it was hard not to look at her without feeling a deep pang in his chest.

He ached for the things she was missing out on not having her mother in her life. It wouldn't be long before she was a teenager, and even though he did his best to tend to her every need, there was a special bond a mother and daughter shared that he could never fill and he knew that. Ivy needed a woman in her life, and even though he missed the closeness and companionship a relationship provided, he just couldn't bear the thought of taking such a huge risk.

Noah caught sight of Hope and her aunt and uncle as he steered their horse and wagon out of the church yard and right on the main road, headed for home. Hope sat on the far right of the seat with her hands clasped together on her lap, staring off into the distance. Of all the women he knew, she was the only one he considered a close friend he could talk to and rely on. He'd bent her ear many times since Maria's passing, and she'd been there for Ivy more times than he could count.

If only they were on the same path. It wasn't as if he'd never considered the two of them as a couple, because he had many times, but Hope's parents made her jaded to the whole concept of love and marriage. Noah, on the other hand, knew the depths of love and what he stood to lose if he went down that road again, and it frightened him more than he cared to admit.

"Are you ready to go, daddy?"

Ivy appeared by his side, and when she placed her small hand in his, he forced the troubling thoughts from his mind and smiled at her. She needed him more than anyone else in his life now, and that was all that mattered. Everything else would have to wait.

* * * *

"I can't believe I'm doing this," Hope remarked.

She grimaced when she saw her friends standing in line at the auction, each of them appearing anxious as they waited to turn over their picnic baskets to Bishop Abram, who was serving as the auctioneer for the event. They were all clothed in what looked like brand-new dresses and bonnets, and they looked excited - giddy even.

"Oh, stop. It's all for a worthy cause. Did I ever tell you this is how your uncle Seth and I met?'

Hope looked beside her at her aunt Sadie, and she attempted a smile but failed miserably. If it hadn't been for her aunt's incessant nagging, she never would have agreed to taking part in such a silly tradition, but she'd come too far to back out now.

"Just look at those single men over there staring at you. I think they're memorizing what your basket looks like so they can bid on it."

Her aunt giggled as she said it, but when Hope saw the gentlemen she was referring to, her heart sank. There was Gabriel, one of the most conceited men in town, who thought he was God's gift to women, and there was Amos, a man three years younger than her who was at least a foot shorter than her too.

There were several other men in the group, but she didn't know most of them. She noticed Noah standing a few feet away, but she doubted he would take part in any of the festivities since he never had before. She'd managed to get out of it over the past four years, but her aunt had such a vise-like grip on her arm, she knew running wouldn't be an option this time around.

"Aunt Sadie, can I ask you something? I want you to be completely honest with me too."

Her aunt gave her a curious look before nodding.

"Am I a burden to you and uncle Seth?"

Her aunt tightened her grip and turned her around so they were face-to-face. Hope could tell by the look in her eyes that her question upset her.

"Of course not. You've never been a burden to us. Why would you even ask such a thing? Has my sister been filling your head with nonsense again?"

Hope smiled. Her aunt Sadie could always sense when something was bothering her, especially when it had to do with her mother. The two women were like night and day and had supposedly never gotten along during their childhood. As adults they merely tolerated each other, but it wasn't as if her aunt didn't try to build a relationship between the two of them. It was her mother who refused to budge.

"We love having you with us, and there's no way I could run my quilting business without you. You've been a Godsend, and don't you dare let your mother tell you any different. Now...get over there and get in line."

She gave her a little push and Hope had no choice but to do as she said. She made her way to the end of the line, literally dragging her feet with every step. If someone like Gabriel or Amos won her basket it would be the longest picnic lunch of her life. Hopefully, someone she could at least put up with for an hour or so would bid on her basket and win.

When Hope inched her way to the front of the line and handed over her basket to Bishop Abram, he looked surprised to see her. "I'm glad you're participating this year, Hope."

She prayed her feelings weren't painfully obvious on her face because she hated to disappoint him. Not trusting herself to speak, she simply smiled at him before making her way back to her aunt Sadie.

There were several other fundraising festivities taking place, and since the auction wasn't scheduled for at least another hour, the two of them walked around admiring the assorted pies, cookies, and other goods for sale. Hope tried not to dwell on the upcoming auction and have fun, especially since social gatherings were far and few between in her little community.

"Looks like Noah will have his hands full deciding who he's going to have lunch with," Sadie said.

Hope followed her gaze to the makeshift stage where the auction was going to be held. Noah stood off to the side of the stage, where he was flanked by three women – Victoria and two other women she didn't recognize. All four of them were talking and laughing, and the women's intentions were obvious by the way they batted their eyelashes at him and stood so close to him she wondered how he could breathe.

"It looks that way," she replied.

For reasons she couldn't explain, seeing the women fawn over him made her uneasy. The thought that he might be interested in one of them brought with it the realization that although they were good friends, it probably wouldn't always be that way, especially if he remarried. After all, what woman would put up with her husband having a close friendship with another woman, no matter how innocent it might be?

"Something troubling you?"

She turned to her aunt, who was eyeing her with an amused look on her face.

"No. Why do you ask?"

Her aunt put her hands on her hips and laughed. "Really, Hope? I have a tough time believing you don't feel a tad bit jealous seeing those women flirt with Noah. You had this same look on your face at church when you saw him talking to Victoria."

Hope's jaw slacked. That was crazy. Why in the world would she be jealous? They were just friends and nothing more. He'd mentioned many times how he wasn't interested in dating again, and...well, there was no way she would risk becoming as unhappy as her mother.

Before she could redeem herself, Bishop Abram was taking the stage and ushering everyone to sit down. Several of the pews from the church had been brought outside for the auction and as Hope and Sadie sat down on the middle row, she noticed Noah making his way to the back, were he stood behind the last pew. He waved at her when he caught her staring at him, and Hope waved back quickly and turned around to face the front, hoping he didn't see her cheeks burning red from embarrassment.

As soon as everyone was seated, Bishop Abram made his way to the podium and the table beside it that was littered with more baskets than she could count. She'd considered the number of single women donating to the auction, but she'd forgotten about the handful of widows, young and old, who might be participating – including Victoria Kaufmann.

Hope searched for her in the crowd and found her sitting near the front. When Victoria turned around in her seat, there was no denying her gaze was centered on Noah as a huge smile spread across her face. Even though Hope wanted to look at him to see what his reaction was, she forced herself not to, especially since her aunt Sadie was watching her every move.

Bishop Abram welcomed everyone to the auction before picking up the first basket – a large red wicker basket that he noted was loaded to the brim with homemade goodies like chicken and dumplings and blackberry cobbler. The bidding started at five dollars, and it didn't take long for the price to climb as several men placed their bids. It eventually sold for forty dollars to an older gentleman named Aaron, who'd been a widower for many years.

When Hope saw Clara, a middle-aged widow, pick up the basket and make her way over to Aaron and sit down, she wondered if she was the only one who detected the sly grin that passed between the two of them. She had to admit it was adorable, and part of her was kind of envious of them too.

The auction continued for at least an hour before Bishop Abram finally picked up Hope's basket. There were only three remaining, and Victoria was also waiting for hers to be called. She noticed Noah hadn't placed a bid on anything, which meant he was probably waiting on Victoria, and that bothered her more than it probably should have. Amos had, thankfully, already bid on and won a basket, so he was out of the bidding, but Gabriel hadn't, and that made her very nervous, especially when he turned and looked her way. The wink he gave her made her nauseous, and she considered running for the hills, but her aunt Sadie wouldn't hear of it.

"The winner of this basket will be treated to a fine lunch, complete with fried chicken, fresh corn on the cob, biscuits, pecan pie, and lemonade. Let's start the bidding at five dollars," Bishop Abram said.

Just as she feared, Gabriel waved his hand in the air.

"Five dollars!" Bishop Abram yelled. "Can I get ten dollars?"

A man she didn't know took the bid, but Gabriel trumped him by bidding twenty dollars. Hope started feeling sick to her stomach. *This couldn't be happening.* The two men kept going back and forth for what seemed like forever, and she could tell that Gabriel was getting annoyed.

"Who is that man?" Hope whispered, pointing to the other bidder. "I don't recognize him."

"He just moved here about a month ago," Sadie replied. "He bought the Troyer's old dairy farm."

Hope sighed. It was bad enough that she might be forced into having lunch with someone as obnoxious as Gabriel, but trying to find something to talk about with a stranger wasn't a fun option either.

"Sixty dollars!" Bishop Abram called.

Gabriel once again raised his hand, and when the Bishop asked for sixty-five, the other gentleman didn't make a move and neither did anyone else. It was the highest bid of the auction so far, which probably should have made her happy, but not under the current circumstances. Gabriel looked her way and the smug grin on his face made her stomach twist into knots.

"Sixty dollars going once, going twice..."

"One hundred dollars!"

Hope inhaled sharply, as did most of the crowd, when someone's voice boomed from the back row. She felt her heart catch in her throat. That wasn't just any voice. She would know it anywhere. Turning slowly in her seat, Hope saw Noah with his hand held high in the air. A hush fell over the crowd, and no one said anything for the longest time, including Bishop Abram, who appeared more stunned than anyone.

When he finally found his tongue again, he called for a higher bid, but no one made a motion to accept it. She glanced at Gabriel, who sat with his arms crossed over his chest and a scowl on his face.

"One hundred dollars! Going once, going twice...SOLD to Mr. Noah Wyse!"

Everyone clapped, and Bishop Abram held out her basket so she could come get it, but she felt glued to the seat. It took her aunt Sadie's prompting – or rather, *pushing* – to make her move, and when she retrieved the basket and turned to walk back, she didn't miss the look of contempt on Victoria Kaufmann's face.

Hope made her way to the back of the crowd and stood beside Noah as Bishop Abram picked up another basket she recognized as Victoria's. She wanted to say something to Noah, but she felt shy for some strange reason and so she stood beside him and waited for the auction to end. To say she was grateful Gabriel didn't win her basket would be an understatement, but Victoria wasn't so lucky. When he placed the highest bid on her basket, there was no denying the disapproving look on her face as she grabbed the basket from Bishop Abram's hands and sat down beside Gabriel on the front pew.

When the auction finally ended, Noah started walking in the direction of her aunt Sadie, which both intrigued and worried her as she followed him. When they approached, her aunt gave her another sly smile, but she rolled her eyes heavenward and chose to ignore it.

"Mrs. Sadie, do you mind if I take Hope home this afternoon?"

His question surprised her, but it didn't seem to faze her aunt, who agreed with more enthusiasm than she expected. When Sadie said goodbye and turned to leave, she didn't miss the little bounce in her step, and she knew without a shadow of a doubt that she would never hear the end of her aunt's gloating as soon as she returned home.

"So, where should we have our picnic?" Noah asked, after turning in his money to Bishop Abram.

Hope looked around the open space surrounding them and pointed to a large pine tree several yards away, which would help shade them from the blinding sun – and, more importantly, keep them far away from Victoria and Gabriel, who were heading in the opposite direction. Once they were settled on the blanket Hope had stowed away inside the basket, the two of them began unpacking the food.

"Noah, you really didn't have to do this. Not that I don't appreciate it, because I do, and I know the kids at the school will too when they get their new books."

Her comment made him smile.

"Oh, that reminds me, where is Ivy?" she asked.

Noah removed the aluminum foil from the plate of fried chicken and set it down between them while Hope poured two glasses of lemonade.

"She's spending the weekend with my parents. She's been begging me to stay with them for weeks now, and I finally gave in, but I didn't want to. The house is too quiet and empty when she's not there."

The tone of his voice made her heart ache, and Hope quickly changed the subject.

"I think Victoria was upset you didn't bid on her basket."

Noah chuckled. "She isn't my type. Besides, Ivy made me promise not to bid on anyone's basket except yours."

Hope almost choked on her lemonade, and she took a moment before she trusted herself to speak.

"That was very sweet of her, but I feel bad you spent so much money. I know how hard you work for it."

When he reached over and touched her hand, it felt...different. Sure, he'd accidentally brushed his hand against her skin many times over the years, but this time the warmth of his touch made her tremble, which had never happened before.

"Don't feel bad. I wanted to do it, and I had planned on doing it long before Ivy mentioned it."

Once their plates were full and Noah said grace over the food, they both started eating, and she was happy to see how much he enjoyed it, especially since she'd spent all morning cooking. They talked and laughed while they ate, and they were still sitting beneath the pine tree long after they finished their meal and the others had gathered their belongings and left for home.

Hope packed the basket and moved it out of the way as Noah stretched out on the blanket on his back and laced his fingers together over his stomach. She followed suit, being careful not to lay too close to him. The last thing she needed was for someone passing by on the main road to see them and get the wrong idea.

She sighed contentedly as she looked up at the pine tree and watched the branches sway with the wind. It was certainly a beautiful day God had blessed them with.

"Hope, can I ask you something? It's kind of personal."

She swallowed past the lump in her throat. "Of course."

When he turned over and propped his body up on his elbow so he could face her, she was suddenly very aware of how close they were. Several different emotions converged on her at once – fear, excitement, anxiety...even longing. She kept her eyes focused on the branches above her to keep from looking at him, worried that her face might betray what her mind and body were struggling with.

"Do you still not believe in love?" he asked.

Surprised by his question, Hope didn't know how to answer at first. "I've never said I didn't believe in it."

He looked at her as if she'd just made a funny comment. "Hope, come on. I know you better than anyone, and you've always made it perfectly clear that you don't want a relationship because of your parents."

She couldn't deny it, but the way he said it made her cringe. Were her feelings that transparent to everyone else she knew?

"Why does it matter so much to you what I believe?"

He sat up and rested his arms on top of his knees. He didn't answer her right away, and he avoided her gaze, but she didn't push him.

"I'm afraid your parents have poisoned your mind, and that matters to me more than you know."

Hope sat up and touched his arm, causing him to flinch in response. "Why?"

When he looked at her, there was something behind his gaze she couldn't quite grasp. Turmoil, maybe? Sadness? She didn't know, but it troubled her nonetheless. They'd had several personal conversations throughout their friendship, but this one was turning into something different...something deeper.

"When Maria died, I thought I would never be able to love again. I closed myself off to the possibility, but lately something's changed. I want that closeness in my life again. I miss it."

A twinge of jealousy caught her off guard and left her momentarily speechless. "I...I think that's wonderful, Noah. You deserve to be happy."

He solemnly shook his head as he peered ahead of him into the distance. "But the one person I feel I could have that with doesn't feel the same way, and I'm afraid there's nothing I can do to change her mind."

The way he stared at her, there was no denying who he was referring to, and the realization shocked her. She wanted to say something, but her tongue felt glued to the top of her mouth. He watched her and waited for a reaction, and all she could think of to do was run.

"We should go," she said.

Hope stood and started gathering her things, but Noah grabbed her arm to stop her. "Hope, please talk to me."

What could she say that wouldn't hurt his feelings and risk her losing his friendship? She honestly didn't know how she felt. Her heart and mind were jumbled with a thousand different emotions and none of them made sense. All she knew for certain was that she wanted to leave.

When Hope pulled free of his grasp and picked up her picnic basket, he hurriedly wadded up the blanket and followed her.

* * * *

Neither of them spoke on the ride to her house, but when Noah pulled up on the reins and brought the horse and wagon to a stop in her driveway, he quickly put his arms around her waist to keep her still before she tried to get away from him.

"Noah, please..." she whispered.

He felt her body tremble, and he wasn't sure if it was from the chill in the air or his touch, but he hoped with his whole heart it was the latter.

"No," he replied. "Not until you hear me out."

His heartrate escalated as the heat from her body sent an electric current coursing through his veins. She nodded in agreement, and he knew he should let her go, but it took every ounce of strength in him to release her.

"If it's your aunt and uncle you're worried about. I've already talked to them both, and they were very happy when I asked them if I could court you."

Hope's jaw slacked, and he instantly regretted not approaching the conversation in a gentler manner.

"You *what*?" she asked, her eyes wide and expressive.

Noah put a hand up to stop her before she flew into a tirade. "I promise I wasn't trying to do anything sneaky behind your back, but I'm determined to make you see that this...*us*...would work. You've just got to have a little faith in love, Hope. Your parents might be unhappy, but that doesn't mean you're destined to be unhappy too. I would never do anything to hurt you. You should already know that about me."

She appeared to be on the verge of crying, and he felt like kicking himself. Nothing was going as he planned, but he couldn't stop now. If he didn't get his point across before it was too late, he knew he risked losing her forever – even as a friend.

Noah gently touched her cheek and let his fingertips slide over her jaw to her lips. "I'm going to kiss you now," he murmured, softly. "Afterwards, if you can honestly tell me you felt nothing at all, then I promise I will let this go, and we'll never speak of it again."

Her eyes widened and she looked terrified, but he noticed she didn't shy away from his touch or try to stop him either. "Noah, no...I've never..."

He smiled as he tenderly cradled her head in his hands, "I know. You've just got to trust me."

When he leaned in close and pressed his lips against her own, he could tell right away how nervous she was by the way her lips quivered, but the effect she had on him was undeniable. His body burned hot with desire, and he felt the insatiable urge to take her in his arms, but he also didn't want to frighten her.

They separated for a moment, but he didn't let go. When she opened her eyes, he hoped he wasn't imagining things and that there was in fact a glimmer of want in her gaze. He didn't have to wonder long as she clutched the front of his shirt and pulled him to her. This time when their lips met there was no hesitation. She kissed him with a longing he hadn't felt in a very long time, and as their kiss deepened, she moaned softly into his mouth and gripped him tighter. When they managed to let go, they were both breathless.

"Does this mean you'll give us a chance?" he asked.

She didn't answer him right away, which worried him, but then he caught her smiling and his fears vanished. "It means I want to take this one day at a time. No rushing. If that's okay with you."

He nodded in agreement, and when she laid her head on his shoulder, he felt a renewed sense of hope that had been lost for many years. God was finally filling in the missing pieces of his life, and he looked forward to what He might have in store for him and Hope...and Ivy too.

Noah pulled her into his embrace and kissed her forehead.

"If you're by my side, that's all that matters to me," he replied.

And it was the truth. As long as they were together, everything seemed possible. Together they could face anything – and he was more than ready for the journey.

A FAMILY FOR RACHEL

STEPHANIE COLLIER

Rachel Conrad pushed her feet against the wooden planks on the back porch as she rocked the sleeping baby in her arms and watched his father plow the pasture behind the house. Under different circumstances, the scene probably could have passed as a picture-perfect family moment, but the sad truth was...it wasn't her family.

She sighed as she looked down at one-year-old Mark Bowman, who was resting peacefully with his chubby little face pressed against her shoulder. It was late Friday afternoon, so it wouldn't be long before she would have to say goodbye and return to her home and face the long weekend, and the thought made her heart ache. When she agreed to help Mark's father, Isaac, care for the infant after his wife passed away six months prior, she never expected to become so attached to him – and Isaac too.

Rachel's gaze drifted once more to the large open field. There were storm clouds lingering on the horizon, but with any luck the rain would hold off until Isaac could finish plowing the last two rows. He pulled up on the reins to stop his horse and plow, and as he removed his hat and splayed a hand through his thick brown hair, Rachel took a couple of deep, even breaths to quell her pounding heart. He retrieved a handkerchief from the pocket of his trousers and quickly wiped his brow before putting his hat back on and signaling the horse to start moving forward again. She knew it probably wasn't ladylike to stare at the handsome widower, but she just couldn't make herself look away.

Much to her dismay, Isaac was the subject of many conversations within the small circle of single women in their Amish community. She had to remind herself repeatedly that she was nothing more than the nanny hired to care for his son, but there were so many nights when she dreamed of becoming more. Perhaps it was foolish, but she believed in her heart that God brought them together for a reason. Maybe someday Isaac would feel the same way.

A rumble of thunder echoed in the distance, causing Mark to stir and open his eyes. Rachel began humming his favorite lullaby to try and lull him back to sleep, and it wasn't long before the soft tune and the momentum from the rocker made his eyelids grow heavy. It also didn't take long before Rachel heard the pitter-patter of raindrops on the tin roof covering the back porch.

She stole another tentative glance at Isaac and was relieved to discover he'd finished plowing just in time before the rain fell. As he steered the horse and plow toward the barn, Rachel stood with Mark and entered the small wood-frame house through the back door. She tiptoed down the hallway to the nursery and carefully laid him in his crib before making her way to the kitchen at the other end of the house.

A few minutes passed before she heard the back door open and close, followed by Isaac's heavy footsteps in the hallway. When he walked into the kitchen, she held a finger to her lips to signal to him that Mark was sleeping, and he gave her an understanding nod.

His hair and clothes were slightly damp from the rain, and she resisted the overwhelming urge to brush away a couple of loose tendrils that were stuck to his forehead. She moved closer so she could whisper without waking Mark, but being near him proved more difficult than she expected it would, and for a moment she couldn't find her voice.

"There's some beef stew simmering on the stove, and there are biscuits in the oven. I'll see you Monday morning."

As she turned to leave, he wrapped a hand around her arm to stop her, nearly stopping her heart altogether. His grip was firm, but not at all rough, and the heat from his touch seared through the thin fabric of her dress and warmed her entire body.

"A storm is moving in, and it's too dangerous for you to drive," he whispered. "Stay and have dinner with me."

His invitation caught her off guard, but she didn't object. Honestly, the thought of sharing a meal with him excited her more than she cared to admit, but she tried to remind herself that from his standpoint it was more than likely an innocent request and nothing more. When she agreed to stay, Isaac went to one of the overhead cabinets and removed two plates and two glasses. She walked over to a drawer in the counter, where the cutlery was located, and took out two forks and two knives and placed them on the dining room table along with a couple of napkins.

He motioned for her to have a seat at the table, and as she sat there watching him move around the kitchen, she couldn't help but notice how happy he appeared to be. Not that he wasn't usually a happy man, but this was different. During the first few months after his wife's passing, she rarely saw him smile, which was, of course, understandable, but it did her heart good to witness him slowly emerging from his shell as he went through the healing process.

Isaac filled their plates with stew and biscuits, and their glasses with lemonade, before sitting across from her. It was the first time she'd dined with him, and she felt somewhat uncomfortable and unsure of what to say or do. After he said grace over the meal, Rachel laid the napkin in her lap and tried to keep her hands from shaking.

"I appreciate you cooking, Rachel. This looks delicious."

She gave him a shy smile. It wasn't in her job description to cook his meals, but she did so out of the kindness of her heart, because she knew he already had so much to tend to with raising Mark alone and trying to work.

"You're welcome. I enjoy doing it."

Her voice cracked, and Rachel cleared her throat and silently reprimanded herself for being so timid. It wasn't as if this was the first time she'd ever eaten a meal with a man, but it was the first time she'd ever felt awkward doing so. If Isaac noticed her apprehension, he didn't mention it. They ate in silence for a long while, but it was a comfortable silence, marred only by the rain pelting the tin roof and intermittent thunder.

"I hope this rain moves out before the festival tomorrow," he remarked.

Rachel furrowed a brow. It was the first time in several days she'd given any thought to the festival, which had been orchestrated by some of the women in the community to help raise money for the King's, a family from their church who'd fallen on hard times. Because of her full-time job caring for Mark, she'd had little time to help with the festivities, but she did donate a couple of her handmade quilts to be auctioned off.

"I hope it does too," she replied. "Were you planning on going?"

She tried to sound nonchalant about it, but the thought of being near him somewhere that didn't involve work made her feel hopeful they could eventually move beyond their employer/employee relationship. Festivals didn't occur very often in their community, and the only other place they both frequented was church, but that wasn't exactly the time or place to socialize on a personal level.

Rachel kept her eyes on her plate, but she held her breath, waiting for his reply.

"*Yah*, I told Bishop Jacob I would help him set up the podium and stage for the auction, so I'll be there most of the day."

Her heart soared, but she contained her excitement and continued taking small bites of her meal, stopping every so often to sip her lemonade. Although her hands trembled like a bashful schoolgirl's, she managed to hold on to her knife and fork.

"I can watch Mark for you while you help the Bishop, if you need me to."

He smiled at her, but he didn't accept her offer right away, which bothered her more than it probably should have.

"My parents are supposed to be there, and they volunteered to watch him for me. You already do so much for us, Rachel. I don't want to impose on you, especially on your day off, but thank you for offering."

She hoped her face didn't portray the disappointment she felt. It was ridiculous, really. After all, this was Isaac's family they were talking about, and she wasn't his keeper or Mark's mother, so she had no right to feel possessive of them.

The heavy rain slowed to a steady rhythm and the thunder dissipated as Rachel focused on finishing her meal. There were so many times when she couldn't wait to see Isaac, but there were also moments that hurt being near him, when the somber reality of their situation gripped her hard and refused to let go. This was quickly turning into one of those moments, and she knew she should distance herself...fast. The last thing she wanted was for Isaac to see her cry.

Rachel wiped her mouth with her napkin and carried her dinnerware to the kitchen sink. Isaac remained at the table and continued eating, which Rachel hoped would give her the chance to slip away easily, but before she could rinse her dishes and make a quick getaway, she heard him push his chair away from the table.

"Rachel, do you mind if I ask you a personal question?"

When he walked over to the sink and stood beside her, she kept her focus on washing the dishes to keep from looking at him. They'd never had a serious conversation about anything other than Mark and his late wife, Julia, so she couldn't imagine what he wanted to ask, but her heart raced while she waited.

"*Neh*, I don't mind. Go ahead."

He pulled up his shirt sleeves and helped her with the dishes, and Rachel made every effort not to touch him in the process. It wasn't that she didn't want to, but she knew even the slightest skin-to-skin contact with him would just weaken her resolve and leave her feeling even more depressed.

"Do you think it's possible for a man's heart to heal after he's lost his wife – to the point where he's able to love another woman?"

Rachel's hands began to tremble again. Part of her wanted to believe that he might be talking about her, but he'd given absolutely no inclination that he felt anything for her other than friendship, and she knew that could only mean one thing – he'd fallen in love with someone else. The realization was like a dagger to her heart.

"I believe God allows our hearts to heal and then expand to include someone else," she answered, softly. "He designed us to love others, and I don't think He meant for that to end, under any circumstance."

Hot tears sprang to her eyes, and she almost choked on her own words, but somehow, she managed to speak without crying. She waited for Isaac to reply, but he never did, and when they finished washing the dishes, Rachel hurriedly dried her hands with a dishcloth and smoothed her apron with the palms of her hands.

"It sounds like the rain has stopped, so I best go before it gets dark. Perhaps I'll see you tomorrow."

She turned away from him and went to the hallway to collect her cape, but unfortunately, he was much quicker. There was an expression on his face she'd never seen before, but she couldn't discern what was going on behind his beautiful hazel eyes, and maybe that was for the best. He held her cape open for her, but he didn't let go right away once he wrapped it around her shoulders. For a moment, she stood with her back to him, enjoying the feeling of his warm breath against her neck. When he released her, she stepped away from him, breaking the connection that was only tightening the vise around her heart.

"Good night, Isaac."

Before he had the opportunity to reply, Rachel opened the front door and walked away.

* * * *

Isaac scanned his surroundings for the hundredth time, but there was still no sign of Rachel. There were people milling about everywhere, and it seemed as if every man, woman, and child from the community was attending the festival...except the one person he truly cared to see. He caught sight of his parents sitting at one of the picnic tables under a grove of oak trees, with Mark in his stroller beside them. He waved when they looked his way, and he attempted a smile, but his heart was heavy.

Where could Rachel be?

"Isaac? Are you ready?"

The sound of Bishop Jacob's deep, booming voice interrupted his thoughts and brought him back to reality. The minister stood nearby, with both hands gripping one side of the makeshift podium they'd constructed for the auction taking place that afternoon. Isaac hurried to join him, and together they lifted the heavy podium and set it in place. With any luck, it would be the last thing the elder needed his help with, because he desperately wanted to take a walk and look for Rachel.

"Are you alright, Isaac?"

He focused his attention on Bishop Jacob, who was now staring at him intently, and he gave him a tentative smile. He really didn't want to get caught in a lengthy conversation over something he was still trying to work out on his own. He trusted the Bishop completely, and there were many times, especially during the last six months, when he'd darkened his doorstep, in search of council or a kind word, but this time was different.

"*Yah*, I'm fine," he replied. "Is there anything else I can help you with?"

Bishop Jacob looked at the completed stage and podium and smiled as he shook his head. "*Neh*, this is perfect. You should get some lunch and spend time with your family. *Denki*."

They shook hands and Isaac left his side and began wandering through the huge crowd of people. All the women had on the same attire, with their long dresses, aprons, and bonnets, so picking Rachel out was no easy task. He felt like kicking himself for letting her leave his house the night before without finishing their conversation. It had been a very long night, with little sleep, and not because Mark kept him up. He'd suffered through many sleepless nights over the past couple of months simply because he couldn't stop thinking about Rachel.

Something changed between them last night that he couldn't quite put his finger on. He hoped she understood he was referring to her when he asked her opinion about loving another woman, but it was hard to read her reaction. When she left suddenly, he felt almost certain she was upset because she didn't feel the same way and she didn't want to hurt his feelings. He needed to talk to her so he could find out once and for all where they stood and if he had a chance. The realization that she might be avoiding him made his heart hurt, and it also hastened his search.

Several people stopped him to talk, but he managed to get away from them quickly. When he reached the last booth, and found Rachel sorting through some jars of honey and homemade jellies for sale, his heart started pounding fiercely, partly from relief but mostly from the mere sight of her.

Her long, wavy brown hair was gathered behind her neck and tied with a satin blue ribbon. She grinned as she talked to the owner of the booth, and her beautiful smile lit up everything around her. It was impossible not to be captivated by her beauty, but there was so much more to her than that. Her compassionate heart, loving spirit, and generous soul were just as beautiful.

Isaac walked up beside her and lightly touched her back, which caused her to jump and almost drop the basket she had looped around her arm. He caught it and held it upright to keep the contents in it from crashing to the ground.

"I'm sorry. I didn't mean to startle you."

Rachel laughed softly. "It's alright." She picked up a jar of strawberry jam and paid the owner for it before placing it inside her basket. "Are you through helping Bishop Jacob?"

He nodded, and they stood in awkward silence for what felt like an eternity before he motioned toward an empty table nearby. "Can I talk to you for a minute...alone?"

She started for the table, and Isaac caught a faint scent of lavender when she walked past him. The aroma wafted through his senses and made him light-headed as he tried to fall in step beside her without stumbling over his own feet and making a fool of himself.

"I owe you an explanation about last night," he said. "I feel like we ended things on the wrong foot."

Rachel held up a hand to stop him from saying anything further. "It's alright, Isaac. You don't owe me anything. I understood what you meant."

It wasn't the reply he hoped for. If she did understand him then he didn't misread her reaction at all, and his worst fear was true – she didn't feel the same way about him. He stuffed his hands inside his pants pockets and shuffled his feet on the ground. It felt as if someone reached inside his chest and placed a chokehold around his heart.

"Rachel..."

She leaned into him, but they were interrupted before he could finish his sentence.

"Isaac! There you are! We've been looking all over for you!"

He turned in the direction of his mother's voice, and it didn't take long before she was closing in on them, pushing Mark in his stroller with one arm and her other arm draped through a woman's he didn't recognize. He felt Rachel move away from him, and just like that, there was a distance between them that felt more like an ocean than just a couple of feet.

When the women reached his side, his mother placed a hand against the stranger's back and nudged her toward him, nearly causing them to collide with each other. Isaac took a tentative step backward and gave his mother a weary look. He knew what she was up to before she said a word, and he felt his temper bristle in response.

"Isaac, this is Ruth Kurtz. She just moved here a couple of weeks ago from one of the communities in northern Lancaster."

He tipped his hat to her, and he tried to smile, but it was a half-hearted attempt, at best. He couldn't be rude because he knew his mother's behavior wasn't Ruth's fault. His parents made comments on several occasions that it was time he moved on, and so far, they'd done everything possible to try and make that happen.

"Oh, I'm sorry," his mother continued. "How rude of me. Ruth, this is Rachel Conrad. She's Isaac's maid and Mark's nanny."

Isaac's blood turned cold as he shot her a resentful glare. She was never one to mince words, but calling Rachel his maid was taking it too far.

"Mother, Rachel *isn't* my maid..."

He wanted to reprimand her, but Rachel kept him from doing so by stepping between the two of them and holding out her hand to Ruth.

"It's nice meeting you," she said. "I hate to rush off, but I really should be going."

They shook hands briefly before Rachel turned to leave, but not before bending over Mark's stroller and kissing his cheek.

"Rachel...please wait," he urged.

She didn't look at him, and when she walked away from them, Isaac felt a piece of his heart go with her.

* * * *

Rachel tickled Mark's stomach as she sat beside him on his blanket the following Monday morning. He loved laying on it and playing with his toys, and in no time, he was cooing and smiling up at her. His laughter was exactly what she needed. The house had been empty and quiet most of the day, which wasn't helping her somber mood in the least bit.

When she arrived that morning, Henry, one of Isaac's farmhands, was there waiting for him so they could make the drive into Lancaster for supplies. Because of this, she and Isaac didn't have time to speak to each other, except for a brief "hello". When the men returned three hours later, they immediately started working on one of the plows, stopping only to eat lunch.

It was probably for the best he remained busy and away from the house – and from her – because she didn't know what to say to him anymore. She felt consumed by a losing battle – not only with his mother's obvious low opinion of her, but from trying to vie for Isaac's attention among the other eligible women in the community.

Within a matter of minutes, Mark fell asleep on his blanket, and Rachel decided to clean up the kitchen while he napped. There wasn't much to tend to since Isaac and Henry washed and put away their dishes when they finished their lunch. Rachel nibbled on her bottom lip as she looked around for something to do. Being idle gave her far too much time to dwell on circumstances she couldn't change, so she tried to stay busy as much as possible.

She wet a dishcloth in the kitchen sink and started wiping down the countertops and dining room table, but not long into her task she heard Isaac and Henry's talking outside. She peered out the window above the sink just as Henry hopped on his wagon and steered his horse toward the main dirt road that would lead him home. Soon thereafter, she heard the back door open and close.

Rachel returned to her cleaning, but with just a few heavy footsteps, Isaac was standing in the kitchen doorway. He remained there while she worked, holding his hat and twirling it around and around in his hands, until he finally stepped inside the kitchen and laid it on the dining room table.

He approached her then, and Rachel sucked in a breath when he stood before her, leaving her no choice but to back up against the counter for support. He was so close she could see the tiny specks of dirt and oil on his cheeks and neck from working with Henry. His sleeves were rolled up to his elbows and the top two buttons of his shirt were undone. He looked rugged, masculine...and determined.

Isaac took the cloth from her and threw it in the sink before grabbing her hands and holding them securely. Her heart raced inside her chest, and her knees shook so badly she worried they might buckle and send her crashing to the floor.

"Is Mark asleep?" he asked.

She cleared her throat and nodded, not trusting herself to form coherent words. He looked down at their joined hands and when he returned his gaze to her again, she noticed he had the same expression on his face that he had Friday afternoon before she left. When he raised her hands, and brought them to his lips, she thought for certain her heart had stopped beating.

"I apologize for being so forward, but now that we're finally alone, there are some things I need to say. I don't want to waste another minute, so please just listen and let me get this off my chest."

She felt a lump form in her throat, and she was thankful he wanted her to remain quiet and let him speak because she wasn't sure she could say anything that might be audible over the drumming of her heart.

"When Julia died, I thought my life would never be the same. It felt like she took a huge part of me with her. Something was missing that I feared could never be replaced. I was angry at God for taking her from me and leaving Mark without his mother. I was angry that He took her instead of me. As terrible as it sounds, I didn't want to live anymore."

Rachel felt her eyes swell with tears, but she kept them at bay, not wanting to upset Isaac any more than he already was. He looked over her left shoulder and out the kitchen window, and his gaze was forlorn and distant.

"When I hired you to care for Mark, I never dreamed it would have such an enormous impact on my life, but little by little I started feeling better, like the broken pieces of my life were coming together to make me whole again. I have you to thank for that."

He looked at her and smiled and she tightened her grip on his hands, not wanting him to let go...ever.

"I think you may have misunderstood me when I asked if you thought it was possible for me to fall in love again. I wasn't talking about another woman. I was talking about *you*, Rachel. But then again, maybe you did understand, and perhaps you don't feel the same way as I do. Either way, I can't let another day – another second – pass by without letting you know how I feel."

He leaned forward and kissed her forehead, and she shivered as the softness of his lips and the heat from his breath lingered on her skin.

"Please don't take to heart anything my mother says. I have no interest in dating Ruth Kurtz or anyone else she tries to set me up with. I know her heart might be in the right place, and perhaps it's my fault because I haven't told her or my father yet how I feel about you. I *will* do that though...and soon."

He bent to kiss her again, but his lips bypassed her forehead and rested instead on her cheeks. She closed her eyes and enjoyed the feeling of his lips brushing against her nose and caressing her face. She expected him to kiss her lips, but he never did, and when he stopped and leaned back to look at her, she became suddenly aware of her ragged breathing.

"If you don't feel the same way about me, Rachel, I will try to understand, and I'll never speak of this again. I promise. I don't want to jeopardize our friendship in any way, but I do need to know if I stand a chance. You mean so much to me...and Mark too. I hope you know that."

He touched her chin before sliding his fingertips over her jaw and down the side of her neck. By this time her chest was rising and falling in rapid succession and she gripped the countertop behind her to keep from swooning.

"I do know that, Isaac. I feel the same way about you. I'm so sorry I overreacted the other day. I thought you were talking about falling in love with another woman, and it broke my heart. I didn't know what to say or do. I just knew I had to leave before I started crying, because I couldn't let you see me that way."

He held her head in his hands and this time when he leaned in to her, he pressed his lips against her own. His mouth was hot and demanding, and Rachel let go of the countertop and clung to him instead. The power he yielded was unlike anything she'd ever experienced before, and when they finally separated, she was so overcome with emotion she had to remind herself to breathe.

"Will you stay and have dinner with me tonight? I want to cook something for you. One of my specialties."

Rachel nodded. "I would love to, but you don't have to do that, Isaac. I can prepare something. You've been working so hard, and..."

He silenced her by kissing her again, but this kiss was gentler than the one before it. His lips barely brushed her own, but it had the same impact.

"I want to do this for you," he continued. "I still have some work to finish in the barn, but I'll be back as soon as I can get away."

She couldn't speak, so she simply nodded, and after one last kiss, he was picking up his hat from the dining room table and heading for the back door. Rachel remained in place, leaning against the kitchen counter for the longest while, not trusting her shaky legs to carry her very far. She could still feel his kiss, and as she traced her fingertips across her lips, she closed her eyes and smiled. Her dream was coming true, and she couldn't remember a time when she'd ever felt happier.

The sound of Mark whimpering prompted her to move, and she went to him and picked him up from his blanket. She kissed his little face and twirled him around a couple of times, which made him laugh. It was such a beautiful sound, and one she would never tire of. Her heart soared when she imagined the three of them becoming a family and never having to face another long weekend in her empty home. It was enough to bring tears to her eyes.

Rachel carried Mark to his nursery so she could change his diaper. She looked forward to sharing dinner with Isaac again, especially since she'd never had a man cook for her before. There were so many new experiences taking place – each one more exciting than the one before it. She felt light on her feet and she couldn't stop smiling. It was a wonderful feeling.

As soon as she changed Mark's diaper, she heard the creaking of the back-door hinges as someone opened it, and she slipped on Mark's shirt and pants before picking him up.

"Let's go see daddy. He must have forgotten something."

With a spring in her step, she left the nursery and bounded down the hallway, but it wasn't Isaac who greeted her when she turned the corner. Much to her surprise – and dismay – it was his mother.

* * * *

Isaac put his sandpaper down and stepped back to examine his work. It took longer than he expected to repair the broken plow handle, but it was coming together at last. The sound of a horse whinnying caught his attention, and he furrowed a brow as he looked toward his two horses in their stalls at the opposite end of the barn, where they were busy eating their grain.

Isaac put the sandpaper down on his work bench and went to one of the windows facing the house, and his heart fell to his feet when he recognized his parents horse and carriage in his driveway. Rachel's horse and wagon, on the other hand, were gone. He muttered a few choice words under his breath as he raced toward the house and burst through the back door.

He heard his mother's voice as soon as he entered the house, and he found her sitting at the kitchen table, bouncing a giggling Mark up and down on her knee. He searched the rest of the small house, but Rachel was nowhere to be found.

"Where is Rachel?" he asked.

His mother stopped playing with Mark and finally acknowledged his presence.

"I sent her home."

Isaac felt his temper rise, and he took a couple of steady breaths to try and remain calm. "You did *what*?"

She stood and walked with Mark to the living room, leaving Isaac no choice but to follow her.

"I told her she could go and that I would take care of Mark. It was almost time for her to leave anyway, wasn't it? Really, Isaac, I don't know why you keep her around. There are so many women in our community who would love to marry you, and you need a partner – not a nanny. I mentioned to her that she might want to start looking for another job soon. I can watch Mark for you."

Isaac closed his eyes and shook his head.

"Mother, I love you, but you don't have the right to choose who I should and shouldn't marry. I have no interest in Ruth Kurtz or any of the other women you've introduced me to."

She rolled her eyes heavenward before sitting on the sofa.

"Oh, stop being ridiculous, Isaac. I'm only trying to help you."

Isaac walked over and stood in front of her. "If you want to help me, then you need to accept the fact that I love Rachel, and I plan on asking *her* to be my wife."

Her jaw slacked open and her eyes became wide and expressive. "Rachel? Well, why didn't you tell me? I thought she was nothing more to you than your employee."

Isaac shook his head again. He loved his mother dearly, but there were times when she could be too crass for her own good.

"I've never thought of her that way. She isn't a *servant*, Mother. I love her and Mark loves her, and that's all that matters." He sighed. "I need to find her. Please stay here and watch Mark until I get back."

Before she could object, he was out the door and taking the reins in her carriage. He steered the horse onto the main dirt road and veered to the right, in the direction of Rachel's house. Thankfully, he didn't have to go far before he came upon her in her wagon. He yelled her name, but the sound of pounding hooves on the gravel drowned out his voice. Isaac ushered the horse to go faster, and within seconds he was pulling up alongside of her. As soon as she saw him, she jerked up on the reins to bring her horse and wagon to a stop and Isaac followed suit.

He noticed right away that her cheeks were wet with tears, which made him even angrier at his mother for intervening. He jumped down from the carriage and climbed aboard her wagon so he could sit beside her.

"I'm so sorry, Rachel."

He wiped the tears from her cheeks before pulling her into his embrace.

"I don't think your mother will ever approve of me."

He frowned. She sounded so tired and defeated, and it broke his heart.

"My mother has never been one for gentle words. I don't understand why, but please don't take it to heart. She's always been that way – with everyone."

She let go of him and leaned back in the seat, but he held on to her hands and rubbed them gently to try and keep more tears from falling.

"She didn't know how I feel about you, but she does now, and I apologize for not telling her sooner. Please don't give up on us. I won't let this happen again. You have my word."

He kissed her lips, and the brief contact was enough to send a jolt of heat rushing through his veins.

"I would never do that, Isaac. I can put up with anything or anyone for you – even your mother," she replied.

Her comment made him laugh out loud, and when she grinned at him, he felt his spirits lift.

"Then come back to the house and let me fix that dinner I promised you. With any luck, my mother won't be staying long, but if she does, we'll get through it together."

She nodded in agreement, and he kissed her one more time before returning to his horse and carriage. As they both turned around and headed in the opposite direction, he looked up at the sky and mouthed a short prayer of gratitude to God for bringing Rachel into his life when he needed her the most. He knew without a doubt in his mind that Julia would be happy for him and Mark too, and that filled him with a profound sense of peace he hadn't felt in a very long time.

He'd stumbled across the answer he longed for, and it was Rachel. Because of her, he'd discovered it *was* possible for his heart to expand and find love again...and he couldn't wait to spend the rest of their days making memories that would last a lifetime.

AN AMISH WINTER

TERRI DOWNES

Summer, 1905

The air was finally beginning to clear. Somewhere overhead, a bird began to sing, as though assuring the world it remained unmoved by present circumstances.

"Are you leaving with the others?" Jacob asked.

Mary looked down at her hands, twisted in her lap. "My family want to go," she said.

"I don't blame them," said Jacob. "But do you?"

"How could I stay without them?" asked Mary quietly.

Jacob was silent for a minute.

"You know what I would suggest – what I would ask," he said.

Mary did not reply. She knew.

"I know that, after everything, you may have trouble..." Jacob paused. "Trusting."

Mary leaned back, taking her weight on her hands, feeling the dry grass beneath them. She nodded, as though only to herself. Jacob looked at her, his expression indescribably sad.

"I'm so sorry," he said. "About everything. Everything you've been through. But I hope – I have to hope, and I have to ask now, while I can – "

The bird stopped singing.

"Do you trust me?" he asked. "Could you... trust me?"

***

Two months earlier

"Mary, are you listening?"

"What?"

Mary tilted her head towards her brother, though she did not look up from the furrowed piece of ground that she had been staring at as though she were preparing to interrogate it.

"I said we should be getting at least five bushels per acre," said Paul, waving his arms expansively as he indicated the field before them. "I knew *daed* was on to something with this winter wheat. I bet everyone else is wishing they had joined in when he suggested combining resources for the first year."

"Some of them did," Mary pointed out, scuffling at the ground with the toe of her boot. "The Kauffmans and the Yoders have those few acres on the eastern side, by the windmill. Everyone else is focused on their cattle raising."

"More fool them," said Paul. "If it doesn't rain soon they're going to have problems – meanwhile we're nearly ready to harvest. And the windmill's finished just in time, too."

He nodded to himself. Mary was not sure whether it was her irritable frame of mind causing her to be unfair, but she thought he looked a little smug. He, and their eldest brother Albert, and their father, had all been looking a little too smug ever since they had started construction on that windmill.

They had only arrived in Iowa in September, along with twenty-one other Plain families who had all moved over from Pennsylvania, arriving over the course of a few months. Many had been from their old community. Most of the families had settled themselves with cattle ranges, breeding from the stock they had brought with them across the country. Mary's father had had a different plan. As soon as they had arrived, he had busied himself with buying up vast areas of fertile land and planting it with winter wheat. Albert had expressed his concerns over whether they would be able to plant in time, as they only got everything sorted by the beginning of winter when the temperature was beginning to drop. But a slightly delayed first frost and perfect winter conditions meant that now, coming up to Summer, they were looking forward to a bumper crop of wheat, and did not have to join in the worries of their neighbors over the recent lack of rain.

"Daed was right," reaffirmed Paul happily as they started to make for home, the small white farmstead in the middle of the plain, distinguishable from any other houses within view by the tall shape of the windmill standing near it. "The risk was worth it, all the loans, everything. We'll pay them back in no time."

The loans.

Mary could not help but glance sceptically at her brother as they walked. Did he know? Had her father told him? Or had it been a secret between him and –

"Samuel!" called Paul suddenly.

Mary stopped short, feeling for a moment as though Paul had pulled the name from her head. Then she focused her thoughts and realized that Paul was waving at two figures cutting across the pasture to their right.

"Jacob!"

Paul waved at the two men as they approached. He sent a smile in Mary's direction, which Mary felt herself obliged to return. He would of course expect her to be pleased to see Samuel, and she did not want to give her feelings away. Not yet.

"Evening," said Samuel, as he and Jacob came onto the path alongside Mary and Paul.

Jacob smiled in greeting. He and Samuel, both young and unmarried, had become good friends on the long journey to Iowa, and now went nearly everywhere together. One might have thought they were brothers, if not for the fact that they looked nothing alike. Where Samuel was fair, with corn colored hair and light blue eyes, Jacob's complexion was muddy, his hair a dingy red.Where Samuel was strong and well-built, Jacob was lean, looking as though he had grown too tall for his strength. He carried himself as though he had just woken up, as though he were waiting to stretch.

Samuel had been the most handsome man Mary had ever met, she had known so as soon as she had seen him at their first gathering before the big move. His bearing and manner seemed to carry the assumption that people would look at him – but he had looked at Mary, at that first meeting, and smiled.

He was smiling now. Mary looked away.

She was determined to act normally, but she was having trouble collecting her wits as Samuel fell into step alongside her. As though they were already engaged, as though everything had been settled. She felt him looking at her – could he tell that she knew?

"I haven't seen you in a few days," he said, softly enough that it was obvious he was speaking only to her, but loud enough that the others could hear. Mary blushed. He really was being far too obvious – wasn't he? Maybe they did things differently in his old community, but in hers, courtships were quiet things.

"Did you two know how well the wheat is doing?" she said, deliberately catching Paul's eye and smiling as she spoke, which she knew would set him off. It did.

"Oh yes," he said excitedly. "Five bushels an acre at least!"

He started explaining the plans they had for harvest, and how they had been working to get the mill ready so they could grind the flour themselves.

"Will you be selling us your crop to grind, Jacob?" he asked. Jacob's family, the Yoders, had been one of the only two families to take Mary's father up on his offer of land and seeds. They had only planted a couple of acres, on the edge of the land Mary's father had bought, but they would surely benefit from the success of the wheat.

Jacob smiled in that way he had, as though he was thinking of something privately funny. "Maybe," he said. "I wasn't sure whether I should keep the whole crop or burn some of it so I can use the space for corn."

"Corn?" exclaimed Paul, with the attitude of a man who had been farming for decades and knew everything there was to know about the subject. "You'd need a miracle to grow corn in this weather. You're much better off keeping the wheat and letting us grind it. The windmill's nearly done, you know."

Mary was starting to feel embarrassed. As pleased as she had been to find their family settled and prospering so soon, this attitude of her brothers and father seemed too close to pride to allow her much comfort.

"I heard," Jacob was saying.

"We were actually headed over to take a look if we could," said Samuel.

Paul nodded, and seemed about to launch into a description of the brand new windmill, but Mary spoke first.

"You can't," she said.

The boys all glanced at her.

"Why not?" demanded Paul.

"It's getting dark."

"What's that got to do with anything?"

"Weren't you listening to *daed*?" Mary felt her tone becoming sharp, and tried to sound more indulgent. "You can't take a candle or a lantern into the mill."

"Oh, right..." Paul looked a little crestfallen.

"Why?" asked Jacob, still smiling.

"It's the flour dust in the air," explained Mary. "It can catch fire."

"Flour catches fire?" he said, sounding intrigued. "I didn't know that."

"Not by itself so much, not when it's in a sack or a bowl. It's only when it's floating in the air, I think because the fire can get to all the little pieces individually..."

"I never knew," said Jacob. "Did you know that, Samuel?"

"Of course," said Samuel, who had been giving sidelong glances to Mary as she had been speaking. Rather than expounding on the topic, however, he changed the subject.

Mary was again unsure of whether she was simply in a more suspicious frame of mind than usual, but she was certain, as she looked at Samuel, that he had not known. That he was lying to seem clever.

This was going to be a problem, she realized. How could she go courting with a man whom she could not trust?

And even Jacob and Paul, walking along and listening to Samuel – Mary kept looking at them, and wondering – *did you know, too? How many people knew about this before I did?*

Mary clenched and unclenched her fists as they walked. Something would need to be done.

*****

"How did you find out?" asked Mary's mother, her brow creased.

"Mrs. Yoder mentioned it," said Mary. "In passing. Though – forgive me – but I can't see that that's the most important point here. When were *you* going to tell me?"

Mary's mother hesitated, and glanced at her father. He was standing at the window of their front room, staring out across the yard and the space beyond, towards his new windmill.

"We – well, we thought – " began her mother.

"We thought we would wait until you had had a chance to get to know Samuel," said her father, turning from the window and facing his daughter. His expression was calm and earnest. "You were getting on so well with him, we thought it might make you uncomfortable to know that he was the one who lent us the wheat money."

Mary frowned a little, turning this over in her mind.

"Yes," she said, "but *he* knew that he had lent the money. He had information I didn't..."

"Goodness, Mary, you're not negotiating a business deal," laughed her father.

"It's not as though *you* owe him anything," said her mother.

"Yes, I know that..." said Mary slowly, hesitating.

She was having trouble remembering her original objections. She had been deeply shocked when Jacob's mother had casually referred to the loan Samuel had given to her father, the one that had allowed him to get the crop planted in time, the success of which had then enabled him to secure a second loan for the construction of the windmill.

She had immediately thought back to the way that Samuel had approached her that night he had first invited her out for a drive. He had been smiling, the way he always did, with that calm assurance that she had so often admired. But had he been so assured because he felt that she did, in fact, owe him something for her family's success?

There were so many questions she wanted to ask. When had her father first asked Samuel about the loan? Had it been before or after Samuel had started smiling at Mary, seeking her out and engaging her in conversation? Had it been Samuel's idea not to tell Mary, or her father's?

And had her parents' encouragement of her courtship with Samuel been because they thought the two of them were well suited, or because they felt obliged to the man?

But now, looking at the reassuring smile her father was showing her, Mary could not bring herself to ask. It might sound as though she was accusing them of – what?

So she nodded. "I understand," she said. "I just feel foolish, acting in ignorance."

"We're sorry that you feel that way," her father said kindly. "It wasn't our intention."

Mary told him that she understood, and agreed that they would not mention her knowledge to Samuel just yet. Then she excused herself, saying that she had to see to her chores.

When she walked outside into the front yard, she found her gaze drawn to the windmill. It soared up against the sky, its four sailcloths giving the unsettling impression of outstretched arms. With the sun setting behind it, all she could see was its shape in shadow.

***

Mary could not think of a real reason why she should drop her courtship with Samuel. The points her father had made were sensible, and the liking she had felt for Samuel was genuine. Perhaps secrecy really had been the best thing, she considered, else she might have been confused as to whether her feeling had sprung from gratitude or from real admiration.

Yet, she found herself avoiding Samuel. Not entirely – they still went for rides, and walks. But she never asked when they would see each other again. She never pushed for extra time together, or told him that she had missed him.

He did not seem to notice the change. Mary tried to convince herself that this was simply because he was confident that she liked him, and not because he did not care whether she did or not. She tried not to count the number of times he actually asked for her opinion.

She spent the afternoons before their scheduled drives going over potential topics of conversation, trying to talk herself into feeling more comfortable than she did by pre-planning the time they would have together.

On one such afternoon, as the sun was sinking over the wide plains in a haze of orange, she was so far gone in her thoughts as she completed her chores in readiness for her evening out that she failed to notice Jacob approaching across the back yard until he was level with the porch. When she saw his long sunset-cast shadow fall across the steps she jumped, sending a puff of flour into the air.

"It's only me," said Jacob, holding his hands up in front of him, his shoulders in their slightly relaxed slouch like always. "Are you all right?"

"Fine," said Mary, placing a hand to her heart, then pulling it away and glancing down in irritation when she saw that she had smeared flour on the neck of her dress.

Jacob watched her, one side of his mouth quirked in a partial smile. Mary shook her head at her thoughtlessness and smiled back.

Something about the openness of his expression made her feel more calm than she had in weeks – since learning of the loan.

"I'm just here to arrange getting my grain milled," said Jacob, walking up the steps. "Your father's agreed to buy my crop. Seems funny, seeing as how I bought the seeds from him in the first place, but we'll all profit in the end, I'm sure."

"You're not going to try corn, then?" asked Mary.

"Not with the weather the way it is."

They had had barely any rain in the last month, and the almanacs were predicting a very dry summer.

"Maybe you could try next year," said Mary. "Or you could alternate the wheat with a legume crop."

"That's a good idea," said Jacob thoughtfully. "And I'm trying to think of ways around the water problem."

"Like what?" asked Mary. It felt good, she realized, to be speaking like this. Discussing important, practical things, things that would reward you for the thought you put into them, instead of winding your concentration around ideas like love and betrayal and gratitude.

"Irrigation, maybe. There's a brook running alongside the my land, between mine and the Kauffman's, you know, and I thought I could use it for the fields. It's still flowing, even without the rain."

"I know the one you mean," said Mary. "I think it's ground water, from a spring, so you don't have to worry about the rain. Will the Kauffmans do the same on their side?"

"John's still ill," said Jacob, shaking his head. "And the oldest boys are having trouble handling things on their own."

"Perhaps you could do it for them," said Mary.

Jacob considered this, and smiled. "Of course," he said. "I should have thought of that."

"I'm sure you would have," Mary assured him. Although she wanted to keep talking, she knew that Samuel would be coming by soon, so she turned her attention back to the table in front of her.

"What are you doing?" asked Jacob, not moving.

"Kneading dough," said Mary, raising an eyebrow.

Jacob laughed. "No, I can see that, I just wondered why you were doing it out here on the porch."

"It gets too hot in the kitchen at this time," shrugged Mary. "We still need to put up shutters to block the afternoon light, but the boys are all busy getting ready for the harvest."

"Ah. I thought you might be using the sunlight instead of a lamp in case you set fire to the flour," he teased.

Mary rolled her eyes. "Only if you throw the flour over the lamp," she said.

"I'll have to try that sometime," Jacob said. "I keep trying to imagine what you were describing, but it's difficult."

"Hmm..." Mary glanced at her kneading. She was just about done. "Hold on."

She went back into the kitchen and came out with a candle in a holder, along with a bowl of water. She handed Jacob the bowl, then set the candle on the far end of the table and lit it.

"Right," she said. "This looks better at night, but for once there's no breeze, so I might as well show you now. Have the water ready in case I make a mistake."

Jacob nodded eagerly, looking for all the world like a schoolboy. Mary could not help but smile at his expression. She took a small handful of flour, then stood at arm's length away from the candle and cast the flour carefully over the flame.

A ball of fire blossomed out from the candle, reaching up and engulfing the falling flour in a flash of light which disappeared into a wisp of yellow flame.

It lasted only a second, but left an after image of light burning in Mary's eyes, forming a bright haze around Jacob's face as she looked up at him to gauge his expression. He looked completely entranced.

"That was amazing! Can we do it again?"

"One's enough," said Mary. "Getting overexcited is how accidents happen."

"All right," he said reluctantly. "Then – "

"What are you doing?" a voice called from across the yard.

Mary and Jacob turned to see Samuel striding toward them. He did not look pleased.

"I was just showing Jacob how the fire reacts with the flour..." began Mary, but she trailed off as Samuel's face remained set in a scowl.

"I asked to see," said Jacob, keeping his voice light. He glanced at Mary. As she met his gaze, she shook her head slightly, indicating that he did not need to stay and defend her. He hesitated for a moment, then said, "Well, I'd best catch your father before he heads off."

Jacob disappeared into the house. Mary tried to smile at Samuel, but she was thrown by his still-angry expression.

***

The next day, Mary sought out her parents once more. She had spent half the night thinking about the decision she had to make, but it was getting harder and harder to ignore the way her heart was turning.

She felt as though she had been caught up, off her feet, for the months she and Samuel had been courting. Caught up by his good looks, by his confidence, by the fact that he seemed to favor her over any other girl in their new community. Even the fact that he had come from a different community within Lancaster had added to his appeal; unlike young men such as Jacob, Mary had not ever known Samuel as a boy, but only as a man.

It had taken the shock of finding out about the loan to shake her from her trance. She had started having doubts – and then, with her newly opened eyes, finding more things to doubt about. She had started to notice how little they ever spoke about her, the two of them. It was always Samuel leading the conversation, and Mary trying to show him how interested she was.

And yesterday... he had gone on about her candle trick for almost half of the buggy ride they had taken. "It's not safe, you were just showing off, think about how you'd behave if you were running a home," and on and on.

Mary had tried to explain that she had done it before, and had even apologized, admitting that it had not been the most sensible thing to do. But he had not let up. And eventually, Mary had started to wonder... was it what she had done that had annoyed him? Or the fact that she had done it for Jacob?

She had thought about how happy Jacob always was to see her, how he sought her smiles and opinion... how friendly they had been back in Lancaster, and how she barely saw him these days, since she had been seeing Samuel. And she had wondered.

She left this latter concern unspoken to her parents, as she could not be sure of Jacob's feelings for her, or Samuel's feelings about those feelings, but she explained that she had misgivings about Samuel's character.

She had been nervous about broaching the subject, as her parents had both been so pleased by Samuel's courtship, but they both sat and listened to her speak without interrupting. In fact, Mary watched her father nodding thoughtfully and began to think how good it was of him not to object to this, given what he owed Samuel and how careful he was bound to be not to offend him. She was going to say as much – but her father spoke first.

"Now, Mary... are you sure that you are not reacting too strongly?" he asked.

Mary looked at him.

"You don't want to make a mistake," he said. "Are you sure you've thought this through?"

His voice was calm, his expression kind. His eyebrows were raised.

As though he knew better than her. As thought he knew that she was simply being over emotional, and that she did not know her own mind.

Mary felt something cold spreading at the bottom of her chest.

"I'm quite sure," she said, keeping her voice steady, even as fear began to make itself known. He could not have misunderstood what she had been saying. So why was he questioning her?

He had always trusted her in the past. Always. He knew that she respected his authority, and had never challenged her unnecessarily over the fact. He had always told her how proud he was of her intelligence, and how she could work things out on her own.

Surely he would not...

But he did.

"Well, I would rather you allowed Samuel to go on courting you," he said. "For now. Something might change, you know. You might realize you were wrong."

Mary spoke quietly. "I don't think I will, *daed*."

Her father's expression closed. "Well, I want you to try," he said. And nodded, sharply. And then left the room.

Mary turned to her mother – who was already turning away.

"*Mamme*?" she said.

"Trust your *daed*," her mother said. "He knows what's best."

Mary left the room without another word.

***

"What's the problem?" asked Albert. "If you don't like him, break it off."

He grabbed the side of the bin in front of him and gave it a shake. "This one's secure!" he called up to Paul on the next floor. "Try the hopper."

"Which one's the hopper?" Paul yelled down.

"Where you put the grain in," Albert yelled back. "You'd think with how excited he is about this, he'd remember what everything's called," he commented to Mary.

He and Paul were double checking the workings of the windmill before they started the harvest. They had already checked the sailcloths; the shafts, pinions and spindles; and the two huge stone millwheels.

"That's what I wanted to do," said Mary, "but *daed* thinks I'm making a mistake."

She did not tell him the shadowed suspicions in her heart, that their father was insisting she keep Samuel happy because of what they owed him. She did not want to sully her father's image in the eyes of his sons; nor, indeed, did she want Albert to become angry at her for suggesting such a thing.

"Hopper's fine," said Paul, as his feet appeared on the ladder above their heads.

"Well then, either you're wrong or *daed's* wrong," said Albert.

He led the way back outside, into bright sunshine that made Mary squint. The sun was still relentless, the sky obstinately blue, the air baked to a crisp every single morning. Many of the families in the area were beginning to wonder what they would do if the rain continued to stay away,

"Right," said Paul, following them out. "You'll find out soon enough."

He looked back up at the windmill. "A lot of people are going to be buying our flour," he said. "Especially now they haven't been able to plant much themselves."

"It's a shame," said Albert, not sounding too concerned. "It's turning into a real drought now, I don't know how everyone's going to manage. I think we'll be the only ones around here who'll have had any success this year."

Mary felt herself becoming desperate. If only they were not all so caught up in this wretched windmill business. She could not remember any of her family being so distant and unfeeling as this before. She was beginning to wish that they had never even come here, that they had just stayed home in Lancaster. All this talk of crop yields and profits... it felt so wordly. Even though the windmill was approved technology, her father and brothers were so obsessed with the thing that Mary felt that they might as well have gone and bought one of those new motorcar things that everyone seemed to have had in the towns that they had passed through on their way here.

"Listen. It's just that I think *daed*... likes Samuel too much," she pressed on. "As a... friend. And I think he might not realize that were not suited."

Albert dragged his gaze away from the sailcloths, which were currently immobile as the mechanisms were all in place now and should not be turned when there was nothing to grind.

"And what do you want us to do about it?" he asked, as though conceding a huge favor.

Mary swallowed down her irritation. "Just... there are a few people who knew Samuel, from his community, back in Lancaster," she said. "Who knew his family. You're all working together in the harvest – just, if you could ask them, in passing, what they think of Samuel. What they know of him. Something."

Albert sighed. Mary turned to Paul. "Please," she repeated, hoping her younger brother would be a little softer.

Paul looked at Albert. "I don't mind," he said.

Mary took that as a yes.

***

She left things at that, for a little while. She did not have to think too much about seeing Samuel, or indeed her father or brothers, as they were all busy dawn til dusk with the harvest. And she kept herself as busy as possible, so that at least half the times Samuel tried to see her she could tell him that she was in the middle of something.

As the days passed, the ground remained dry, the plains wide and brown under the sun as though they had been scorched by it. The cattle farmers were beginning to become seriously worried. Some even began to speak of returning to Lancaster. Mary's father greeted this news with annoyance, and Mary could not help the uncharitable thought that he was angry not because he might lose his community, but because he might lose his customers.

She repented of the thought after she had had it, but it left its shadow behind.

When Samuel mentioned to her, one evening, that he had also been considering whether staying was the right option, Mary almost panicked, thinking that he meant to propose, that he wanted them to wed and return to Lancaster together. She quickly began to speak of the last dry summer she had experienced, when she was seven, and how everyone had felt then, but that the rain had come anyway, and that if they just remained faithful in prayer –

She realized, as she spoke, that Samuel was not really paying attention. She did not mind, as she was just trying to keep the subject changed. They were walking back to her home, and had almost reached the yard gate, and soon she could say good night.

As they reached the gate, she turned to say goodnight, hoping to cut off any ideas of him coming inside with her. But as she did so, she caught sight of something.

"Oh, look!" she cried excitedly, and pointed.

Over the long line of the horizon, a cloud was rising. Just one, by itself, but it was no wisp that would blow away in the night. It was large, substantial, and heavy, with a darkness underneath the pink caused by the setting sun that hinted at the possibility of rain. Rain, at last.

"It's a cloud!"

"I can see that," said Samuel, sounding a little amused.

Mary ignored him, looking out at the cloud with as much satisfaction as if she had made it herself. She hardly noticed Samuel beside her, looking away from it.

But then he glanced down at her. And as she reached out to open the gate, he reached out to stop her, placing a hand on the latch. And the other hand on the small of her back.

Mary felt a jolt up her spine, and stepped away with a jerk, turning so that her back was to the gate. She stared at Samuel. He looked quite calm – had she made a mistake? But he reached out again, to her shoulder, and ran his hand down to her elbow. His expression was soft, a smile playing on his lips. Mary almost wondered if her reaction was unwarranted.

But he was not – he was not supposed to do this. He was not allowed. Mary took a deep breath. Whether his old community had different rules or not – and, really, how different could they be, now that she thought about it – she had not given him permission to do this. They were not engaged. They were not married. He had no right to touch her.

She pulled her arm away. Samuel raised an eyebrow. It looked like a challenge.

What can I say? Mary wondered. *What can I say to make him leave? Please, please, leave –*

And then she heard them. Footsteps. Louder than they should have been, on the dust of the road, or perhaps that was because Mary was so happy to hear them.

"Jacob," she said, unable to keep the relief from her voice. She caught Samuel's frown, but did not care, as Jacob approached with his easy smile.

"Evening," he said, but Samuel was already turning around.

"Evening," he replied. "I have to go."

"Oh, all right – " Jacob hesitated as he found himself speaking to his friend's receding back.

It may have been Mary's imagination, but she thought she saw a flicker of something, as Jacob watched Samuel leave. Something cold. Something hard.

He turned to Mary, his face creasing as he apparently noticed her distress.

"What's wrong?"

"Nothing," said Mary. Lying. She swallowed. "How have you been? Have you managed your irrigation project yet?"

Jacob nodded, still looking as though he wanted to press her for details. But she smiled encouragingly, and he began explaining the work he had done on his and his neighbor's fields.

"It worked so well that I did end up burning some of the wheat so I could plant other things there," he said, leaning his forearms along the top of the gate and craning his head forward to see past the windmill to their right. "Vegetables and so on, things that can grow in the fall."

"Was that this week? I wondered what the smoke was," said Mary.

"I did it in sections, keeping it under control, you know," said Jacob. "I remembered your candle demonstration, I didn't want to risk the windmill going up."

He smiled. And Mary felt the warmth of knowing that he had acknowledged her input. That he was showing her he respected her.

And that he wanted respect in return. Why else would he have come to tell her that he had done as she said and helped his neighbors? He had no other reason to come over.

Mary found herself smiling back. She knew, now, after this evening, that she could never be with Samuel. And when that was done, then who knew? Maybe Jacob...

"Do you know what was wrong with Samuel?" Jacob was asking.

"We just... had a disagreement," said Mary carefully, leaning against the gatepost and looking out at the darkening sky. "Things are a little strained."

"Right..." Jacob glanced toward the house. "Is that..." he stopped.

"Is that what?" asked Mary.

"I was wondering. Um..."

Mary began to feel worried. Jacob was not meeting her eyes. "What is it? Tell me."

"I don't want to overstep," he said, still looking away. "I thought maybe your father had already cleared everything up, when I saw you with Samuel. But then, if you're unhappy about it all – "

"What all?" asked Mary. He was not making any sense.

He looked up, then. Surprised.

"The... you know, about Samuel?" he coughed. "Your brothers were asking around, and one of the men – you know, Eli Miller, he said he had heard a rumor a while back, and he didn't want to spread it but if they were worried..." he trailed off.

Mary was still staring.

"They told your father," he said. "A few days ago. Did he not tell you?"

"No." Mary stepped toward Jacob so she could look him right in the eye, through the settling darkness. "Tell me."

Jacob swallowed. And he told her.

And Mary felt her insides turn to ice.

***

"You don't understand."

"Obviously not," said Mary, her throat tight. "I'm asking you to explain it to me."

They all looked upset. Her father, Paul, Albert. No, not even upset – annoyed. Annoyed that Mary had called them from their work and was pestering them with questions when they had better things to do.

"If there had been any substance to that rumor," her father said through gritted teeth, glancing out through the front window, "of course we would have told you. But we saw no reason to upset you with something that might just be lies."

"But it might have been true," hissed Mary.

Outside, the sky was low and gray, the cloud from the evening before having been joined by a mass of others. There had been no rain, but there was a warm wind gusting hard across the fields, whipping the grass into long, snaking waves.

The men her father had helping him put the grain through the mill would be working frantically to keep up the pace, Mary thought. And her father and brothers obviously wanted to join them. But they had not gone yet. And she knew – she knew, somehow – that this meant they had been caught out. If they truly believed there was nothing to worry about then they would have gone back out to work.

"But that girl wasn't pregnant," Albert pointed out, his mouth twisting distastefully as he said the words. "Obviously."

"She might have lost it," Paul said quietly, though the other two glared at him for this.

"Whether she was or not," said Mary, "the fact that there was reason to think she might have been speaks for itself."

"She might have been lying," said her father.

"Why on earth would she lie about that?" Mary snapped, just managing to stop herself from shouting the words.

She glanced at the door, wishing she had waited for her mother to return from the Yoders' before starting this conversation. Surely she would have understood. But then, would she not have been told the story along with her father? Would she not also have chosen to ignore it?

A low rumble of thunder shook the house. Mary felt herself anticipating the tapping of raindrops on the windowpanes, but none followed. Just more dry wind, more waiting, more frustration.

"We don't know any of these people, from Samuel's old community," her father pointed out. In his calm, collected manner. "We had no reason to think badly of Samuel. Why would we believe such a rumor without proof?"

"I believe it," Mary said.

That, finally, got her father's full attention. Her brothers also looked away from the frantically turning windmill, their expressions matched in horror.

"Mary – you didn't – you and Samuel – "

"What? No," Mary said, shocked in her turn. "*No.*"

"Then why would you – "

"It wasn't – I mean, there were moments." Mary closed her eyes briefly. "When I could tell. If I had let him, he would have."

It had not just been that touch, last night.

It had been in the way he looked at her. His eyes raking her up and down, stopping where they should not. The way he had sought her away from everyone else, the way he blocked her when there were other people present. The way he treated her as though she were already his.

She had chosen not to notice. She had not wanted to.

"How could you not tell me?" she asked quietly.

And then, because if she was ever going to feel justified in asking this question, it was now:

"Was it because of the money?"

And her father would not look at her.

"Was it worth it?" she asked, her voice almost a whisper.

"The windmill," she heard Albert say.

She covered her face with her hands. "Stop it."

"No, the windmill – "

"*I don't care about the – *"

"No, look!"

Albert was pointing, frozen, his face the color of ash. Pointing outside. Across the yard, and the pasture beyond, to the windmill. To the men running away from it. To the thin, dark stream of smoke rising above.

***

"I wondered where you were."

Mary looked up, shielding her eyes, even though the sky was still purpled with clouds. They were still irritated from the smoke, as were the insides of her nose and throat, and she did not want to open them at all. But she managed to smile at Jacob, who looked even worse than she did. He sat down next to her and took off his shoes as she had, joining her as she dangled her feet in the stream. His stream.

He had come running, yesterday. She had seen him from the back pasture, where she had run to with her family once they had realized that they would not be able to put the fire out. Paul and Albert had had to forcibly drag their father away to stop him from trying to get back and save his beloved windmill.

They had run until they heard the explosion of flames behind them which signaled that the flour-filled air inside of the mill had caught. Mary had glimpsed it from the corner of her eye as she had looked behind her; a sudden rush and roar of brightness leaping into the sky.

They had watched as the structure had been eaten away, blackening and crumbling. The fire had spread to the sailcloths, which continued to whip themselves around in the wind, billowing flames and smoke in their wake, flinging burning debris as far as it would go. Onto the dry grass of the next pasture. Into what was left of the wheat fields. Onto the house.

And Jacob had come running, sprinting toward the fire. Dragging them back with him, as the fire and smoke followed them across the dry fields. Back to his home. The only safe place – because, as he had told Mary, he had, just that week, burned a large strip of his land to prepare it for planting. And fire will not burn across something that has been burned already.

Mary's mother had met them as they arrived, her eyes wild with fear. They had stayed standing outside the house, catching their breath, coughing, watching in the distance as everything they owned turned to ash, praying for the rain to start. But the clouds had remained obstinate and aloof, and the fire had continued its path until it petered out at the edges of the wheat fields.

"Have they found out what caused it yet?" Mary asked now.

Jacob shrugged, and covered a cough. He and the others had used the water from his spring to dampen the ground around his house, just in case, and he had had to spend a lot of time in the way of the wind-driven smoke. His skin still looked a little gray, and Mary could smell that he was several baths away from ridding himself of the odor.

"Might have been lightning," he said. "Or the speed of the wind. If there was a piece in the mechanism that hadn't been properly oiled, it could have sparked."

Mary nodded. "To be honest," she said, "I don't really care. And – and I'm glad its gone."

She wondered if she would have to explain herself, but Jacob was nodding. Someone – probably Paul, she thought – had filled him in. On everything.

"I'm sorry for your family's losses," he said, "but honestly – me too."

They paddled their feet for another minute. The air was finally beginning to clear. Somewhere overhead, a bird began to sing, as though assuring the world it remained unmoved by present circumstances.

"Are you leaving with the others?" Jacob asked.

This morning, there had been an emergency meeting called. All the families. There had been talk already of leaving, of heading back to Lancaster. There was no blessing here, some had said. Even if there was rain, now, it would be such hard work to keep going. It was too much. They were ready to leave.

Others had wanted to stay. Jacob's fields had been saved, as had the Kauffman's. A few other families seemed on the fence, each seeming to want someone else to make a firm commitment before they followed. There were five in all. Not that many. But enough for a start.

Mary looked down at her hands, twisted in her lap. "My family want to go," she said.

"I don't blame them," said Jacob. "But do you?"

"How could I stay without them?" asked Mary quietly.

Jacob was silent for a minute.

"You know what I would suggest – what I would ask," he said.

Mary did not reply. She knew. Hers had been the first name he had called, as he had run to them the day before. Hers had been the hand he had held, pulling her to safety. She was the one he had come to, over the course of the afternoon, to check on. To reassure.

There was no hiding it now.

"I know that, after everything, you may have trouble..." Jacob paused. "Trusting."

Mary leaned back, taking her weight on her hands, feeling the dry grass beneath them. She nodded, as though only to herself. Jacob looked at her, his expression indescribably sad.

"I'm so sorry," he said. "About everything. Everything you've been through. But I hope – I have to hope, and I have to ask now, while I can – "

The bird stopped singing.

"Do you trust me?" he asked. "Could you... trust me?"

Mary closed her eyes. She thought about her father. Her brothers. Samuel. The men who she had trusted before.

And then she thought of Jacob. Showing her such care and kindness even when he thought they she could never be his.

And, on her smoke-singed, upturned face, she felt it. The first fat, wet raindrop, hitting her so hard she could hear it against her skin. And another. And another.

The bird flew off, presumably excited about the prospect of worms. And Mary and Jacob stayed where they were. The rain fell harder, and Mary blinked drops off her eyelashes. She caught Jacob looking at her. And smiled.

"Yes," she said. "I do."

THE AMISH DIVIDE

MONICA MARKS

Samuel

Samuel wiped the sweat from his brow and sat back on his heels to admire his handiwork. The crib was one of beauty and while simplistically crafted, the miniscule detail was a credit to his attention. *I hope the Chandlers will be happy with this,* Samuel thought to himself, rising to his feet with agility but even as he thought it, he knew that they would be more than content with his latest project. The Chandler family had been customers of the Bender family for generations and even after Samuel's father had passed the previous spring, the Chandlers had continued to use Samuel as their carpenter despite his young age and relative inexperience.

"I understand if you would rather use another craft man, Mrs. Chandler," Samuel had said not long after his father's death. "I haven't nearly business which my father had."

Miriam Chandler had shaken her head vehemently.

"Oh no, Samuel! Carpentry is in your blood. You are an artists and artists don't need to paint a thousand pictures to be wonderful. You are a natural. My family will continue to use you and I am certain that the others on the community feel the same as I do. Do not fret, child. You and yours will not be forsaken during this time."

"I appreciate the sentiment, Mrs. Chandler but we will be fine," Samuel said with a slight twinge of anger. He did not want the pity of his congregation. *They see us a charity mission,* he had thought but the reality was, despite their newly orphaned status, the Bender children were very well revered in their small Pennsylvania district. Samuel genuinely was a gifted tradesman, something his father had done very well to ensure from the time the boy was young. Mrs. Chandler had not been fibbing; Samuel had a natural talent for working with wood. It went deeper than his ability to work with his hands. He had an affinity with the trees and could often be found wandering through the gullies when the long work day was completed. It was not uncommon to see him conversing with the long-standing beasts, explaining the plans he had for them, how much good they would be doing for the people in the future. Samuel was a gentle soul and it reflected in everything he did. He was the second oldest child in his family and while his oldest sister Greta tended to their small animal farm, Samuel was afforded some freedom to earn extra wages with his woodworking. The two youngest children, Zachariah and Sadie were still in school however, after the death of their father, they had made themselves indispensable to their oldest siblings handling light chores and cooking. It was God's blessing that their aunt and uncle lived moments away via carriage and often offered their assistance with the youngest children. *We are so fortunate to live in such a place where death brings us closer rather than tearing us apart.* When Samuel's father had taken ill, both the family and community had bound together and helped prepare the siblings for the inevitable. The road had been painful and slow but by the time the oldest living Bender had succumbed to his fate at the young age of forty-seven, leaving behind four mourning children. Regardless of the hardships they had endured, their relationship had thrived and grown as a result.

"Samuel! Samuel, are you out here?" Greta's voice piped through the workshop and Samuel turned to face his sister. She rounded the corner and looked at him.

"Yes, Greta. Is all well?"

"Yes, supper is ready. I just wanted to make sure that you didn't lose track of time again. Yesterday you stayed here well into the night working and didn't eat a morsel."

"I just want to make sure that this cradle is perfect for the Chandlers," Samuel protested, standing back so his older sister could see his completed project. She nodded admiringly but put her hands on her hips disapprovingly.

"It looks lovely but that is no excuse for poor diet. Zachariah and Sadie depend on you and we can't afford for you to become ill. You must be more conscious of how much you are eating. You will fade away if you are not careful."

Samuel laughed and followed Greta out of the small structure, wiping his hands on his slacks.

"I don't think there's any fear of that," he replied but he understood her concern. He was losing weight on his already slight frame. Greta grunted.

"Don't laugh, Samuel. It isn't funny. *Daed* lost a lot of weight when he got sick, remember? It makes the younger ones worry about you."

Startled, Samuel stopped in his tracks.

"What a terrible thing to say, Greta! I am not sick!"

"I know you're not but Sadie and Zachariah make the connection that you are losing weight as papa did. They are young and it makes them worry. You spend far too much time in the woods and not enough time caring for yourself."

Slowly, Samuel nodded and continued walking after her toward their modest home. *She is right. She will be married soon and I will be left to care for them alone when she moves to another district. I must be more aware of how they see me.* As they approached the house, Sadie met them at the back door, bouncing from one foot to the other in excitement.

"What is it, Sadie?" Samuel asked with some alarm. Her small face broke into a beam.

"Nothing!" she squealed. "The Chandlers had their baby! A little boy! And they named him after you, Samuel!"

A feeling of warmth and happiness swept over Samuel. He shot Greta a glance and they grinned at each other.

"Now you see? It's a good thing I stayed up late to finish the crib." Greta shook her head begrudgingly.

"Wait! Where are you going?" she demanded as Samuel turned back toward the workshop.

"Didn't you hear Sadie? The Chandlers had their baby and named him after me! I can't have them waiting for their cradle or they'll regret their decision!"

"Samuel! Not before you eat! Samuel!" But her younger brother was already halfway across the property, either ignoring or unhearing Greta's pleas. *I must rush this over to the Chandlers right away! I hope it does not disappoint them. I wonder if one day I will make one like this for my own children. Maybe I should think about finding a mother for those children first.* Samuel chuckled to himself, his smile overtaking his face. As he hurried into the shed, his heart bursting with pride and elation, he did not notice the figure standing behind under the giant pine, watching him in the gentle hue of twilight.

Willa

She ducked swiftly as the glass flew directly at her head and tried to steady her trembling hands before she slowly turned. Her father's rage stained face glowered at her from across the table.

"You will sit down this instant!" Seth Albrecht was incensed but Willa was long accustomed to these violent outbursts.

"I will return when you have calmed," she answered with a nonchalance she did not possess. Her heart hammering, she quickly walked out the door, expecting a blow to reach her before she had a chance to exit the room but it did not materialize. Willa hurried toward the ravine at the rear of the property. How Seth handled her perceived insolence would vary from day to day. Some days he would allow for her to leave without incident whereas other times, removing herself from the situation would result in a fate worse than death. On occasions when Seth did not follow, Willa would return home as if there had not been a dramatic scene mere hours before and he would be the same loving, doting father whom she had adored since childhood and she would eagerly accept his good mood. But the dreaded times when he did chase after her, she knew that it was in her best interest to stay away for the night for once she returned home, the beating would be merciless and no amount of pleading or cajoling would help.

As she reached the outskirt of the gulley, she paused behind a coniferous tree to glance back at the house and exhaled in relief. Seth had not come outside. She would be safe to go home that night. The previous week she had spent the night in the Flickinger barn where Mr. Flickinger had discovered her in the morning. He had shooed her out of the horse stall with a pitchfork as though she was a diseased hobo, ripe to rob him blind. Willa had grown up in the district with these people and attended worship with their sons and daughters but she was not one of them. Willa was the only child of Seth and Sara Albrecht. Her father was a candlemaker and her mother a seamstress, often catering to the English. Willa was afforded many luxuries which some of her peers were not such as a toy chest filled with handmade dolls and more outfits than the other girls in the district. It wasn't long before the Albrechts were being reprimanded for spoiling young Willa.

"You must think of having siblings for her. She is becoming too good for the other children. You can see it in the way she acts," the Bishop warned them when Willa was five. The bishop did not understand that Sara had taken extreme caution not to produce more children with her husband in fear for their safety. Instead, Sara had curtly told him that Willa was not spoiled and if the other children felt inadequate, it was the fault of their parents and not of the Albrecht parenting. After that, the Albrechts became outcasts in their own home. No one had any idea what was occurring behind closed doors and in fact, Seth was often regarded as the victim in the circumstance.

"That poor man. Married to a shrew who treats their daughter like an English princess," the gossips would say behind their backs. "He shouldn't allow for Sara to spend so much time in town doing work for those people. It is affecting their way of life."

The members of the community did not see the bruises on Sara and Willa's bodies as Seth rarely struck in the face and they spent so little time paying mind to the women that the signs of domestic abuse were lost upon them. It was easier to disregard the women as uppity than to delve deeper into the true story. When Willa was thirteen, Sara abruptly disappeared. At first, Willa was certain that Seth had murdered her but there was absolutely no proof to that effect. Willa desperately tried to find evidence that he had harmed her mother but as a year passed, Willa was forced to realize that her mother had simply had enough and had fled. Seth fell into the role of abandoned husband with sociopathic ease and relished the attention which the district bestowed upon him. He gobbled down their sympathy with humbleness, accepting the outpouring as if he deserved it. It was around this time that Willa realized that her father was not of sound reasoning. The eligible women made it clear that they were there for him, bringing meals and cleaning his home. Their brazenness made Willa sick to her stomach, especially when she knew what kind of man they were pursuing. She was still young enough to believe if she spoke, she would be heard and she desperately tried to forewarn everyone about Seth. Of course, she was again regarded as mean spirited and disregarded.

"What kind of cruel child says such awful things about their own father when he is going such a trying time? This is what happens when you spare the rod," the community squawked. Little did they know that when Seth caught wind of his daughter's warnings, the rod was not spared, not in the least. The beatings became more and more intense but with every blow, Willa grew stronger somehow, against the odds. When Willa turned fourteen, Rose Slagel began spending more and more time at the Albrecht home and the teenager knew that she could not stand to watch the naïve, idealistic Rose become Seth's next victim. It did not help that Rose genuinely wanted to befriend Willa. The younger girl knew that any attempt to dissuade Rose from becoming ensnared in Seth's trap would be an exercise in futility. So, with a heart filled with fear, Willa packed a small bag and followed in her mother's footsteps one night, disappearing without a trace. Her brave journey took her into the big city where she lived on the streets for several months, begging for money. There were several options for a young, innocent girl in a morally bankrupt world but Willa managed to scrape by without resorting to any form of activity shunned by God. When the weather turned bitter, Willa's homespun clothing and little street smarts did nothing to protect her from the concrete jungle. The people became more aggressive with the cold, recognizing their own survival at stake. Her safety was compromised constantly and fifteen-year-old Willa was in a constant internal battle with herself. *Is this better or worse than living with father? Am I more or less safe here? Where will I die first?* The need for food and shelter won out and with her tail between her legs, she was forced to return home. Seth allowed her but only if she was baptized immediately. Malnourished, friendless and out of options, Willa agreed. Following the baptism, she was severely beaten and starved for three days. Seth forced her to sleep in the woodshed all three of those nights without a blanket. She would have been warmer on the streets and likely better fed also.

A few years passed and Willa continued to endure the abuse by the hands of her father, unbeknown to anyone, including Rose Slagel whom Seth had married in Willa's absence. It gave Willa some relief to know that Rose was safe from Seth but she often wondered why. The answer came when Rose announced her pregnancy at the end of the second year. Soon after the baby was born, a premature girl, that Rose began to receive the same treatment. *He wants a son!* Willa finally realized.

"Willa, you must leave here. I will get you some money. You are young and have your entire life ahead of you. But you must leave this place," Rose urged her one morning after Seth had left for his workshop. Willa had snorted contemptuously.

"Oh? And where will I go? I almost died on the street once. Why don't you go? It isn't too late for baby Lucy."

"I cannot leave here. I have my family. Lucy needs her father."

"And I don't need my father, Rose?" Willa shot back furiously. She knew she was being unreasonable, that her step-mother was trying to protect her but she suddenly was just as angry at Rose as she was at Seth. *Why didn't she just listen to me? Why didn't they just all stay away?* She thought mournfully. It was too late. Seth had claimed another victim.

As Willa wound her way through the very familiar pathway, she started to wonder if Rose was right. Perhaps she should leave. There was nothing in the community for her. Her skills as a seamstress were mediocre and she was not apt to be married as she was a pariah in the district. She had no friends, no family. She desperately wished she knew where her mother had gone but of course there was no way to find that out without money, money which she did not have. Willa turned toward the Bender farm and stopped by Samuel's workshop. Willa peered inside and saw that no one was inside. Content, she leaned heavily against the huge pine overhanging the small structure and dug into her apron pocket. Her hands closed around a tin which she pulled out. Inside the nondescript case were two hand rolled cigarettes and a pack of matches. Immediately, she lit one and inhaled deeply. The sun was beginning to set and Willa felt her stomach grumble. Seth had started just as they were to sit down to dinner meaning that Willa was going to spend another evening without food. Suddenly she heard a voice call out.

"Samuel! Not before you eat! Samuel!" Willa dropped the cigarette and ducked behind the tree as Samuel Bender came striding confidently toward her hiding spot, a serene smile on his beautiful face. Willa felt a pang as she looked upon his face. Samuel had always been one of the few people in the community who had been kind to her despite her wretched reputation. If she had thought it possible, Willa would have believed that she had a deep seeded affection for the man. *Well if there was anyone in this district I could care for, I imagine it would be Samuel Bender,* she told herself, watching with relief as he opened the door to the woodshed, apparently not seeing her. Willa waited, unmoving until he walked out a moment later, a wooden cradle in his arms. Willa felt her heart begin to quicken as an obscure thought crossed through her mind. *I wonder if he will make one of those for our children.* Before she could stop herself, Willa fully exposed herself and called out.

"Samuel!"

Greta

"You seem elsewhere, Greta. Is everything all right?" Ivan peered at his fiancée but she did not seem to hear him. Her hazel eyes were focussed on her brother, her stomach churning with some unidentifiable emotion.

"Greta!" She jumped and looked at Ivan.

"Dear Lord, Ivan, I am sitting right here. No need to scream in my ear!" she admonished as she took his arm. They rose from the sitting room and headed outside to join the rest of the congregation.

"I tried speaking to you normally but apparently, you seem to have selective hearing. Why are you staring at Samuel like that?" Greta narrowed her eyes.

"Like what?" she denied. Ivan laughed and shrugged.

"Don't play coy with me, *liebchen.* I can see the way you're staring at your brother. What is going on? Are you quarrelling?"

Again, Greta stared at Ivan as though he were crazy.

"Quarreling? With Samuel? Over what?" she demanded. Ivan shook his head.

"I agree, it seems to be a rather odd question as Samuel is hardly one to give you any trouble but I can't help but sense that something is wrong. What is it?"

"That's just it – I'm not sure," Greta confessed, lowering her voice, her eyes trained on Samuel once more. Zachariah and Sadie were at his side and Samuel seemed to be entertaining them and other children with a captivating tale.

"What do you mean?" Ivan pressed. Greta chose her words carefully, trying not to sound outlandish.

"He has been acting slightly...different," she said slowly.

"Different how?"

"I don't know...I can't pinpoint it exactly but there's something evasive about him as of late."

"You have to be more specific, Greta. *You're* starting to sound evasive," Ivan joked.

Greta shook her head and sighed.

"Ever since the night the Chandler baby was born, he has been acting secretive. For example, he says he is out working in his shed and then I go to call on him and he's in the shed but he's not working on anything. He's just standing there guiltily." Ivan blinked.

"Maybe he just needs a break from everyone," he offered. "I can understand that."

"Perhaps," Greta agreed. "But I can't shake the sense that he is hiding something."

"Maybe he is courting someone," Ivan said flippantly but Greta nodded, looking grim.

"That's what I'm afraid of," she confirmed.

"Why? He's of an age where marriage should be on his mind," Ivan told her reprovingly. Greta sighed.

"I agree. I'm not concerned that he courting someone. My concern is who he is courting."

Greta had discovered Samuel's secret by accident. Zachariah had been sent home from school due to a fever and Greta needed Samuel to watch over the boy while she tended to the vegetables. She could not find her brother in the shed as he had promised to be but instead discovered him in the woods. This was not unusual but aside from the rare red in Samuel's cheeks, there was a fresh cigarette butt on the ground by his feet.

"Are you smoking?" Greta had almost screamed at him. Samuel shook his head vehemently.

"Of course, not!" Samuel had retorted. "What do you want?"

Taken aback by his tone, Greta had looked around in the trees, suddenly sensing that they were not alone.

"Who is out here with you?" she demanded.

"No one," Samuel had answered quickly, covering the space between them. He led his older sister out of the trees.

"Zach is home sick. I need you to tend to him," she told him, looking over her shoulder. She saw nothing but the sense of unease did not disappear. Over the following days, Samuel's behavior became more furtive and Greta's maternal instinct grew shaper. It was not until a week later that Greta finally made sense of what her brother may be hiding. Rose Albrecht appeared on the Bender farm looking troubled.

"Hello, Greta. Is Samuel home?" Rose asked, baby Lucy asleep in her arms. Greta rose from the vegetable garden, her brow furrowed.

"I believe he is in the work shed, Mrs. Albrecht. Is there something I can do for you?"

"I am looking for Willa," the new mother said worriedly. "She has not been home in three days."

Greta felt the blood drain from her face.

"Well I assure you, that girl would not be here," Greta stated indignantly. "Why would you think such a thing?"

Rose's mouth pursed into a line and she reached into her apron pocket. She held out her hand and Greta drew near to see what she held.

"I found this in Willa's room," Rose said simply. Greta took the item and saw it was a hand wooden rose. The workmanship was definitely that of Samuel and Greta could not reconcile the meaning.

"Did your step-daughter steal this from my brother?" Greta yelled. The baby stirred in Rose's arm and the older woman shook her head.

"I do not think so, Greta. I think that Samuel gave this her. And I think he has been hiding her here."

"Outrageous!" Greta wiped her dirty hands on her apron and glared at Rose but the woman stood firm.

"If you are so certain, let's go and have a look," Rose said calmly. "It is imperative that I speak with her."

"Yes, I imagine her poor father is going out of his worry. I will show you. Samuel would never do such a thing!" The women started toward the back of the property. From the treeline, Samuel clasped Willa's hand and pulled her back into the forest.

Samuel and Willa

It had started without either one realizing what was happening. The night the Chandler baby had been born, Willa had called out to Samuel and it was as if the two had seen each other for the first time. Samuel had spun at the sound of his name and looked into the cornflower blue eyes of the district "bad girl." Perhaps it was the way the sunlight captured her light brown hair in the dusk or the naked look of pleading in her face, begging him not to walk away. Something about the way Willa stood there in the shadow of the majestic pine, her arms at her side plucked a chord in Samuel's heart and he found his pulse quickening.

"Willa! What are you doing out here?" he asked. She shrugged slowly and walked toward him. Instinctively, Samuel looked behind him at the house and then back at Willa. She immediately recognized the gesture and froze. *He is worried that someone will see us together. No one wants to be seen with the district outcast.*

"I -I'm sorry. I should go," she stammered, humiliated and turning back toward the trees.

"No! Wait! Come back here. I am just surprised to see you here. Are you all right?"

Unsure now, Willa stood and nodded.

"Yes. I...I was just out for a walk," she lied. A shadow crossed over Samuel's face. Like everyone else in the community, he was aware of the troubled past Willa had faced over the years. It was no secret that she had claimed Seth was an abusive man but no one paid much credence toward the rumors as Seth was God fearing with an impeccable reputation. His kind smile and easy disposition was well known to all. When Sara had ruthlessly abandoned their family, it was unsurprising that young Willa would act out in defiance. However, Samuel could not help but wonder if there was any truth to what Willa had claimed. He could not imagine why anyone would leave their peaceful and comfortable life to live with the English in the streets. There had been rumors that Willa had even been arrested but the details or truth of such a story had never been established. As Samuel stared at the lovely woman in the trees, he was overcome with the doubts which he had possessed previously.

"The Chandlers had a baby tonight," Samuel offered. "They named him after me."

Willa's eyes lit up.

"That's wonderful news! They have been trying to have children for a long while. And they named him for you! That is the highest form of flattery, Samuel!"

Samuel grinned and shrugged modestly.

"I think that they have taken pity on our family since the death of my father." Willa dropped her eyes contritely.

"I was so sorry to hear about your father. He was always very kind to me when I was a girl. Once he made me a wooden pendant. Just after my mother..." she didn't finish her sentence and now it was Samuel's turn to feel saddened.

"Would you like to come with me? I made this cradle for them. I am off to drop it off." Willa shook her head.

"No, I don't think that is a very good idea," Willa mumbled, again retreating into the trees.

"Wait! Don't leave, Willa. I – why don't you stay here in my shed. I won't be long. Unless you have to get home?"

Gratefully, Willa looked at him and nodded eagerly.

"I can wait!" she exclaimed. "I don't need to be home."

Samuel was consumed with a bittersweet feeling. He had a feeling that Willa was in no rush to get home but he was happy she would be there when he returned. True to his word, he was back in less than an hour and Willa was waiting for him by the light of a single kerosene lamp. They spent that night talking into the wee hours of the morning with Samuel sneaking back into the house before Greta woke at dawn. He had no illusions about what his sister would say if she discovered he was hiding Willa Albrecht in his workshop. The following morning, Samuel hurried back into the shed. He was filled with a deep disappointment that Willa had left. He wondered where she had gone. *If she went home, will Seth be angry with her? Will he harm her?* In his distress, Samuel absently picked up a small piece of wood and began to whittle. As his mind turned, his hands created. The morning light spilled into afternoon heat and when Greta appeared at the door to the shop, Samuel dropped the piece into his pocket guiltily.

"What are you doing, Samuel?" she demanded, looking around suspiciously.

"Working," Samuel barked with more anger than he intended.

"On what?"

"What is it, Greta?"

"You are acting strangely. Come inside and eat."

After supper, Willa was back outside the trees as if she was silently willing him to return. She did not know what she was doing there. The previous night, she had left slightly after Samuel had snuck back into the house, wondering what nightmare she was facing in her own home. To her surprise, the family was sound asleep and no one had missed her.

Seth had left for his shed in the morning and Rose had waited for her to wake.

"You must consider leaving here," Rose told her again as she fed Lucy. A flash of annoyance sparked through Willa's body.

"You cannot get rid of me that easily, Rose," Willa retorted, ignoring her step-mother's distressed look.

"You can fight me, Willa or you can heed the advice of someone older and wiser than you. You cannot stay out all night long and not expect there to be serious consequences. Last night I managed to talk him down. Tonight, you may not be so lucky."

"Oh? Am I lucky?" Willa laughed but worry flooded her belly. A small part of her wondered still if Seth had anything to do with Sara's disappearance even though she knew logically that her mother had simply had enough one day. Every day Willa wondered if Seth would go too far. Rose's words only reiterated something she often considered. Willa left the house that afternoon and waited in the woods for Samuel to appear. When he finally did, he led her inside the shed and placed something in her hand. When she opened her hand, it was a hand carved wooden rose. The detail was so akin to the one that Samuel's father had made her years previous that it brought Willa to her knees with melancholy. They spent the evening side by side in the woodshed, their fingers gently tracing circles in each other's palms. Slightly after midnight, Samuel escorted Willa back to her home. Before she scampered off into the dark house, Samuel grabbed her arm.

"Are you certain you're safe?" he asked, staring deeply into her eyes. She looked away and nodded, glancing at the still, dark building. Impulsively, he leaned over and kissed her. Surprised she jolted back. They looked at each other and then Willa beamed. She leaned forward and deposited another sweet kiss on his lips and disappeared into the darkness. Smiling, Samuel headed toward his own home. As Willa quietly crept into the silent kitchen, a blow hit her face without warning.

"Where have you been?" Seth hissed. Shocked, Willa's hand flew to her face.

"I w-was out for a walk," she breathed, backing away.

"Are you acting like a fallen woman? Trolling around in the night?" he hissed, drawing closer to her. Another fist hit her in the stomach and Willa doubled over, gasping.

"Seth! Leave her be!" Rose yelled, running down the stairs.

"You get back to bed and mind your own!" Seth snarled. Willa took the distraction as an opportunity to flee the house, Seth screaming with rage. As she fumbled off into the woods, she saw him lumbering after her in the pale moonlight but Willa knew he would never catch her. She knew the woods much better than he ever would. Rose stood on the landing, trembling, tears streaking her face. On the floor by the bottom step lay an intricate wooden rose pendant.

"Are you chasing after a fallen woman?"

Samuel froze in his tracks as Greta's voice rang out in the darkness.

"Fallen woman?" he asked innocently without turning around.

"Look at me when I am speaking to you, Samuel," Greta snapped.

Samuel spun on his heel and stared back at his sister.

"Why in God's name would you pick Willa Albrecht of all the eligible women in our district, Samuel? You have the world at your feet! You are handsome, intelligent, patient! She is trouble!"

"You don't know anything about Willa, Greta!"

"I know she smokes cigarettes, even though she is baptized and has sworn to follow God's will. I know that she lived on the streets doing God knows what with God knows who. I know she lies and I know she was arrested while fraternizing with the English."

"Oh you *know* these things, do you?"

"Don't be facetious, Samuel. I care about you and I will not have you hitch your star to a wagon not worthy of your time." Samuel was suddenly furious.

"No matter how much you pretend to be, you are not my mother, Greta. I am a man who can decide whom I will or will not marry."

"Marry?" Greta's mouth dropped open. "You cannot marry that woman!"

"That woman has a name. Her name is Willa. Please use it from now on." Without waiting for a response, Samuel ran up the stairs, his heart racing. It was out of character for him to fight with Greta but Willa was a sensitive topic. *Greta doesn't understand Willa is a beautiful person. Inside and out.*

The following morning, he discovered Willa asleep under the pine by the wood shop. He saw the bruise around her eye and she did not leave the shed again for three days. Samuel brought her food and water and stayed with her as often as possible, managing to keep her from Greta's prying eyes. On the third day, Samuel convinced her to go into the woods with him. He showed her how to speak to the trees and she found herself more enamored with him than she had been prior. It was then that they had overheard Rose and Greta in the garden. Samuel pulled her back into the trees.

"We will wait here," he told her, holding her close but Willa shook her head.

"No. I am tired of running," she told him and Samuel looked down at her in surprise.

"You don't have to come, Samuel. I will not embarrass you in front of Greta. I will say I snuck into your shed and stayed here without your knowledge." Samuel scowled.

"You will do no such thing. You are not someone I am ashamed to be with. If you are ready to come forward, I am at your side."

"You will face a lot of backlash, Samuel," Willa warned him.

"You are going to be my wife. There is nothing we can't face together," he answered, hugging her tightly. She stared up at him in disbelief.

"You want to marry me?" she whispered.

"More than anything in the world."

They smiled at one another.

"Are you ready?" Willa nodded and together they headed back toward the shed. They almost collided with Willa's stepmother and Samuel's sister.

"Oh Samuel," Greta's voice was leaden with disappointment. "What are you doing?"

"It's not his fault, Greta," Willa piped in. "I – "

"Willa has been staying in the woodshop," Samuel interrupted.

"Why would you allow for this, Samuel?" Greta asked, shaking her head angrily.

"Because Seth is abusive." Greta snorted.

"Oh, Samuel you are so gullible. She is making up stories for pity," Greta snapped, glaring at Willa. Willa hung her head, tears welling in her eyes. She felt as though she was thirteen years old again and being judged by the entire community, being called a liar.

"No, she's not." Rose spoke for the first time, drawing closer to her stepdaughter. She gently reached out and touched her yellowing eye. Willa drew away.

"Seth hits Willa and I frequently. Sara left because of his abuse." Greta and Willa stared at Rose open mouthed.

"I came to find you, Willa because I went to the authorities in town today and filed a police report. They have arrested your father and I need you to testify. I am worried for Lucy," Rose continued. "Will you please come with me? I have had enough for all of us."

Tears spilled onto Willa's cheeks and she choked on the emotions she was feeling. It was a heady feeling to be believed for the first time in her life.

"Yes! Oh yes!" She threw her arms around Rose who returned her embrace with intensity.

"I'm sorry it took so long. I should have protected you better. But it isn't too late for us." Willa nodded, brushing the tears from her face. She turned to look at her fiancé, her face filled with love.

"Thank you for believing in me," she said as she followed Rose.

"You are my wife-to-be. I will always believe in you," he replied. Rose smiled at the words and Greta stood, silently dumbfounded at the revelations she had just learned. As Rose and Willa walked away, Rose grabbed for Willa's hand and placed the pendant in her palm.